SERPENTI

BOOK TWO OF THE ROYALS

BROOKE SIVENDRA

Copyright © 2019 by BROOKE SIVENDRA

All rights reserved.

The moral right of Brooke Sivendra to be identified as the author of this work has been asserted by her accordance with the Copyright, Designs and Patents Act 1988.

This is a work of fiction. All the characters in this book are fictitious, and any resemblance to actual persons living or dead is purely coincidental.

No part of this publication may be reproduced, stored in a retrieval system or transmitted in any form or by any means, without the prior permission in writing of the publisher, not to be otherwise circulated in any form of binding or cover other than that in which it is published without a similar condition, including this condition, being imposed on the subsequent purchaser.

Cover by Virtually Possible Designs

Ebook: 978-0-6485688-3-4

Print: 978-0-6485688-2-7

ASHER

"*King Asher!*
"*Hail King Asher!*"

Asher's heart was in his throat and his pulse raced as he looked over the crowd. His mouth felt dry, as if it were stuffed with cotton. He was king, and even though he'd known that since he'd learned of his father's assassination, it had just hit him.

His mother's pale face flashed in his mind—then Noah's, his father's, and Abi's.

His spine tingled as he wondered if his enemies were in the crowd, watching him. Or were they in the palace?

Either way, the biggest mistake they could make would be to underestimate him.

He raised his hand again, waving goodbye.

Luke was by his side before he'd even turned away from the podium. "Jesse's on his way home. He has her. Abi is safe."

Asher exhaled, tilting his head back and squeezing his eyes shut.

Thank you.

"They're in the air and they'll be here in a few hours," Luke said. "William Bennett has been informed. Jesse requested she, and the IFRT team with her, be brought to the palace. The Bennetts will meet us here. He doesn't want you at the airport—the security risks are too high right now—and Abi doesn't need any media attention."

"Okay," Asher said quickly—he just wanted what was best for Abi. "What happens now? How is she?" he asked, forcing the questions from his throat as they walked toward his living quarters. A security team walked in front of them, and a second team behind them.

"I don't know the full details yet," Luke said, sounding tired. "Jesse's preparing a full brief that will be given to us when he lands. Jesse will treat her injuries as best he can—"

"What injuries?" Asher asked, his words catching. He'd known she would have injuries of various kinds, and though he didn't know if he was prepared for the full details, he did know he had to find out.

Luke looked sympathetic. They both knew what Abi could've been subjected to. "Again, Jesse didn't elaborate. His primary concern was getting them on the plane, in the air, and out of Adani airspace. He's going to call you in about fifteen minutes."

"Thank you," Asher said, looking straight ahead. His emotions were all over the place. He was exhausted, grieving, overwhelmed, and scared.

So scared.

He didn't know who to trust, and he had no one to ask. His first thought was that he wished he'd had more time to prepare for his new role, but Asher knew that nothing his father could've said or done would've prepared him for this.

He waited for the security team to scope out his living quarters before they entered. Luke closed the door behind them. Asher's eyes went straight to the liquor cabinet, but he refused to let himself go there. He would not be weak.

Luke lowered his voice, like he was worried he'd be overheard. "You need to be aware that we are monitoring Alistair's every move. Additionally, we have tracking devices on him, and his cell phone is tapped."

Asher narrowed his eyes and looked over his shoulder to see the second security team a safe distance behind them. "What aren't you telling me?"

"I'm telling you we don't trust him," Luke said, meeting Asher's gaze. "He lied about when he last saw your mother, and he didn't tell you his allowance had been stripped. What concerns us most is that your father was concerned by his reaction to that disciplinary action."

"Why didn't I know about this?" Asher demanded.

"Your father had a meeting scheduled with you for the afternoon he was killed. He was set to brief you on Alistair's situation at that meeting. He never got the chance," Luke said, his voice strained.

"What was Alistair's reaction to being told about his allowance?" Asher asked, turning away from Luke. He was having a hard enough time keeping his own emotions in check without watching Luke battle with his own.

Luke sighed. "Yelling and storming out of your father's office."

Asher frowned. "Why did that surprise Father? That's exactly the response I would've expected."

Luke nodded. "It was a good act, but it was the look your father caught as Alistair was leaving. Your father said it was a look that said he didn't care—that he wasn't afraid. We don't know what that means. Maybe he thought he'd prove everyone wrong and be back on his allowance within months; maybe . . . maybe there were other reasons he wasn't afraid."

"I don't want him alone with my mother," Asher said, even though it was an order he'd already given. "I don't trust him. I haven't for months. He knew about Abi, and he knew about IFRT. If he is working against me, though, I don't know why he would tell me he knew about my involvement."

Luke paused, seeming to choose his next words carefully. "Maybe it was a slip-up in a moment of rage. Alistair's drug use wasn't just recreational. Over the past few weeks it's become apparent that he's a high-functioning—if you want to call it that—addict. Jesse has been watching him for months and, unfortunately, it's become apparent that Alistair owes money. A lot of money."

"To whom?" Asher asked, narrowing his eyes.

"His drug dealers. They have no apparent connections to Adani, but where there's money, there's drugs, especially cocaine. I'm sorry I don't have more for you," Luke said, running a hand through his hair. They were all stressed, Asher knew. Luke continued, "Jesse was following Alistair's every move before he went to Adani. It's been on hold since. At the moment, we're in survival mode. Keeping you alive is our primary objective; beyond that, everything is taking a back seat."

Asher looked him square in the eyes. "Do you trust your teams?"

"Yes," Luke said, "I trust them. I watched them during the attack, and they did everything they could to help your parents. I lost six men in that attack."

"How did they know my parents would be in that car?" Asher asked, voicing the question haunting his mind.

Luke ground his jaw. "Because someone leaked that information. You asked if I trusted my teams. Yes—for the two teams that are working with me *now*. Do I trust every security guard in this palace? No, I don't."

Asher pressed his fingers to his temple. "How am I supposed to do this? I've had no training, and worse than that, I don't know who I can trust!" Asher raised his voice, losing control of his emotions.

Luke didn't respond with words, but his nod was gentle and understanding. "You have me and Jesse. We have worked for your father since before you were born. Let us look out for you. We will watch your back."

Asher searched his eyes as he silently screamed the words he didn't let leave his lips: *You didn't have my father's back, or my mother's.*

They were interrupted by Asher's cell phone.

"Jesse," Asher said quickly.

"Hey, Ash. I am sorry. So, so, sorry," he said, his voice drained.

"I know," Asher said, his own voice sounding like gravel. "How far away are you?"

"A couple hours. She's okay, Ash. Abi wants to talk to you. I was going to give you a briefing, but I'm waiting for some more information. I'll have it ready by the time we land, and then we'll make a plan to move forward," Jesse said, his words steely with determination.

"Okay. Please put Abi on the phone," Asher said.

His chest burned, and he realized he was holding his breath.

"Asher," Abi said, and her voice had never sounded sweeter.

He exhaled in relief, turning his back to Luke. He needed a moment of privacy.

"Abi," he said, his voice a whisper. "Are you okay?"

He didn't know why he'd asked. Of course she wasn't okay—she'd been held hostage and God only knew what else. But he wasn't thinking straight, and his mind was a tangled web of emotions.

"Thank you for sending Jesse to help them," Abi said. "I'll be okay, Asher. But how are you? I'm so sorry to hear what happened to your father, and your mother. I wish I could've been there for you. I . . . How is she doing?"

A tear slid down his cheek, the first tear he'd shed. She had no idea how much he needed her right now.

"She's stable and fighting." He inhaled a shaky breath. "Tell me about you. What happened?"

She paused for a moment and acrid bile rose in his throat. He didn't want to hear it, but he knew he had to.

Eventually, she said, "I'll give you the full story when I see you, but my car was attacked and I was pulled from it. I was taken to a hut in an abandoned village, and then into a safe house of sorts. I was held there until I was prepared . . . that's what they call the process of cleaning captives and dressing them in lingerie for the men they will be given to. But someone helped me, a brave young girl, and she's with us. I have to help her, Asher," she said, her words a plea.

"Of course," Asher said quickly. "Whatever needs to be done—we'll find a way."

Abi cleared her throat. "I . . ."

Asher noted a tremble in her voice.

"I was being prepared for Lamberi," she said, her voice a hoarse whisper.

Asher felt like he'd been kicked in the stomach, and his hand reached for the wall.

"I couldn't let that happen," she said shakily. "I knew I wouldn't survive and I would never return to Santina if I was handed off to him. Anyone else I could've survived, but not him. I'm sorry, Asher, I don't know what repercussions this is going to have for you. Adani officials are involved and they're not going to be—"

"Stop. Stop," he repeated, gently. "I don't care, I can deal with whatever repercussions there are as long as you're home and safe. Just come home, Abi."

"I'll see you soon," she said. "Be careful, Asher."

He squeezed his eyes closed. Once again she was thinking about him, when he would hardly blame her for only thinking about herself and the ordeal she'd just been through. He would've understood if she'd blamed him for being taken captive.

Prince Asher's girlfriend.

The repulsive, skin-crawling sensation still lingered when he thought of that voice recording. He was part of the reason she was taken. Everyone else had been stripped from him: Noah, his father, his mother. Why wouldn't they have targeted Abi too?

He was so lost in his thoughts that he forgot to respond.

"Asher?" Abi asked quickly.

"Sorry, I'm here. I'll be careful, and you too. Come home to me," Asher said, gritting his teeth.

ABI

She ended the conversation more worried than before she'd called him.

"How did he sound?" Jesse asked, surprising her.

Her eyebrows lifted. "How do *you* think he sounded? You spoke to him too."

They were sitting across from each other on the royal jet. Abi couldn't lean against the seat because her back was missing a few layers of skin from the roof she'd misjudged, and she hadn't even bothered to look in the mirror. She could feel the cut on her lip and another near her temple—where the security guard had knocked her unconscious.

Jesse's eyebrows lifted in response. "I want your opinion," he said.

"He didn't say that much," she said. "He inhaled sharply at the mention of Lamberi's name, which was a fair reaction. But more than that? He seems . . . flat. Tired. Broken, in a sense. How can he not be?"

Jesse nodded. Abi was still learning to read him, but she liked him. His eyes diverted to the clouds as the sun shone through them, lighting them up like a beautiful painting.

Abi asked the question she thought she already knew the answer to. "Do you think I was taken so you could be lured away from Santina?" She grimaced. "If you had been in Santina, instead of in Adani looking for me, would King Martin still be alive?"

"I don't know," Jesse said, grinding his jaw. "We'll never know the answer to that. And even if we could, it wouldn't change anything. I know King Martin, and I know that's not what he'd want me to focus on."

Abi didn't need to study him to know he was grieving. His face was a universe of pain.

"What would he want you to focus on?" Abi asked.

Jesse looked straight at her. "Keeping Asher alive."

Abi swallowed and her saliva felt like shards of glass. "Do you think that's what they have planned next?"

"I'm not entirely sure," he said. "They either think he's incapable and will wait for Santina to fall under his leadership, or they'll attempt an assassination. Either way, the end result will be that they attempt to kill him, because Asher is more than capable. Santina will not fall, not under his watch. And that will only leave his enemies with one option: the same one they had for King Martin."

Abi returned her gaze to the clouds.

"You're a target by association, Abi—that, and Lamberi might make a move for what he thinks is his. We need to plan for all possibilities," Jesse said.

She nodded, but she couldn't ignore the sinking feeling in the pit of her stomach. "Will Asher have a better chance of surviving if I'm not in his life?"

Her eyes locked on Jesse's.

A moment passed, and then another.

"It's too early to know that," Jesse finally said. "And I can't answer that only from a security point of view. Asher has lost two of the most important people in his life, and the third is fighting for her life." He shook his head, then continued, "Look, I know your relationship has been brief, but I'm not underestimating the importance of it. Asher is going to need support now more than ever, and distancing yourself from him may cause more harm than good. Regardless, it's not my decision to make. Asher will be fully briefed and given all security intelligence. He can talk to you, and then the decision can be made from there. It is his decision."

Abi noted what he didn't say. "But you will advise him on what you think is best."

He sighed. "It's my responsibility as head of security. Nothing stands in the way of that. Nothing."

Abi looked at her bloody wrists. They'd been cleaned and dressed but blood was seeping through the bandages. "You looked for Abi Mackenzie and you couldn't find her, right? That's why Asher pushed for my real name."

Jesse met her gaze and he showed no sign of being uneasy. Abi didn't blame him, and she knew his response before he spoke.

"If Asher had a girlfriend, or were to spend more than one night with someone, then yes, it's my responsibility to make sure I know everything about them. I pushed him because my team needed to know, and because he deserved to know."

Abi nodded, diverting her gaze.

"I try not to get involved in their personal lives, Abi, but if there's a security risk, I need to know about it, and I couldn't do that given I couldn't find your true identity. It concerned me, but only for those reasons. On the way home from your apartment the night you told Asher you were a Bennett, Asher asked me what I thought. I told him it didn't concern me, and now I'm telling you the same thing. As long as you pose no risk to Asher, I have no problem with you."

"But you know I lied to him," Abi said quietly.

"I understand the reasons you did, and I understand what you've just been through. If you're thinking I don't approve of you, you're wrong," he said, looking her in the eye. "Asher needs someone who is brave, who can think under pressure, and someone who can connect with people. You didn't make a mistake throughout this entire ordeal, and I'm so impressed by that. I couldn't have trained you better if I'd had months or years to train you for such a situation. Some things can't be learned—they're instinctive."

"I knew what was going to happen at every stage," she said bitterly. "I've spent ten years trying to save those who have been taken. Even though I knew the risks, I still couldn't believe it was happening to me. And when the team didn't come, I thought it was over... I thought I'd never return to Santina until Lenna walked into my cell." Abi exhaled a shaky breath. "She saved my life."

"And you saved hers," Jesse said with a small smile.

Abi looked over her shoulder. Rachel, Daniel, and Lenna were asleep on the lounge chairs.

"Close call," Abi said under her breath.

"It doesn't get much closer," Jesse agreed. "Try to get some sleep."

"Thank you again for coming to help them," Abi said.

Jesse nodded and gave her a tired smile.

ABI AWOKE and a scream roared through her lips. Her hands clutched the seat and it took her a moment to realize where she was. The plane had touched down on the tarmac and Jesse held his arms up in surrender.

"It's okay," he said cautiously, like he was prepared for her attack. "We're in Santina."

She leaned forward, gasping. Fragments of her dream lingered in the dark corners of her mind, but they refused to come back to her.

She ran her palm over her eyes as her lungs fought for breath. With warm cheeks she gingerly raised her eyes to Jesse. "Sorry."

One eyebrow lifted. "For what?"

"Screaming the plane down," she said, straightening. Her back was stinging and it felt wet and sticky.

"You screamed when we hit the tarmac—that's all," he said, seeming to understand.

Abi didn't know what she'd been dreaming about, but she knew it hadn't been a good dream. Unease lingered, and when she opened her jaw, it cracked, causing her to wince.

She looked over her shoulder. Rachel was awake and Lenna was sitting beside her, ready to depart. But their eyes weren't on Abi—they were looking out the window. Abi craned her neck to see what they were looking at. On the tarmac stood teams of security guards, lined in rows.

"Your parents will meet us at the palace," Jesse said. "They're with Asher now. I requested no one meet us here because the last thing you need is to be photographed stepping off a royal plane. Until we have more information, I think it's best if you keep a low profile."

Abi nodded. She just wanted a hot shower and to see Asher.

King Asher.

So much had changed in a matter of days.

Jesse stood as they continued to taxi to the hangar and retrieved a blanket from the overhead cabinet. "Put this around your shoulders. It's going to be cold."

"Thank you," Abi said.

She draped the blanket around her, ignoring the sting on her back. She hadn't seen the wounds in a mirror, but she knew it wouldn't look good. She wasn't going to dwell on it, though—she wasn't in Lamberi's hands, and that was all that mattered.

"Also, I don't want you walking on that ankle for a few days," Jesse said, digging his teeth into his bottom lip. "The ground staff have a pair of crutches, but it'll be hard to navigate the steps from the plane with them. I'll have two of my men help you down, if that's okay?"

Abi held her tongue. The last thing she wanted was to be carried down—the last thing she wanted was to be touched by men she didn't know—but the sooner she was off this plane, the sooner she could see Asher.

"Okay," Abi said, sounding less than enthusiastic. Jesse gave a sympathetic nod.

They'd had an awkward conversation about her injuries, and she wondered if he still thought she'd held back information. She'd told him she hadn't been raped. Cavity searched—yes. Her breasts fondled—yes. Intercourse—no.

She'd lied to Asher once, but lying wasn't a habit of hers, and it was a mistake she wouldn't repeat.

The plane came to a stop and her team was by her side. Abi looked into Lenna's wide eyes and took her hand. "We're going to be okay, I promise."

Lenna nodded, but she looked far from sure.

Rachel said, "Daniel and I can help her down the stairs and into the car."

Jesse nodded. "Okay." He pressed on his ear lobe and then said, "Copy."

He held out a hand and motioned for them to go ahead. Rachel and Daniel moved in and Abi laid her arms around their shoulders. She was intending to hobble, but they all but carried her out. Lenna stayed close, like a shadow.

They were swiftly escorted into cars, and as they drove through Santina, Abi looked through the window like she was seeing it for the first time. A part of her had given up hope that she would ever see Santina again, and now as they wove through the streets, she took it all in and cherished the beautiful city she'd been born and raised in.

She was home.

ASHER

*A*sher extended his hand to William Bennett. The man's grip was firm, but not crushing.

"Have a seat, please," he said, gesturing toward the sitting room chairs.

A servant brought a tray of tea and sweets, and security guards lined the walls of the room and neighboring hallway. Asher had barely been able to go to the bathroom without being watched.

"How is Emilia?" Emma asked.

Asher cleared his throat. "The same. There's been no change in her condition; however, the doctors have said she's stable, and that's a good sign. Other than that, they said it's a waiting game."

Emma nodded, her eyes glistening. "Can . . . can I see her tomorrow?"

Asher looked between Emma and William Bennett. Emma was an open book, but William was closed off, his face impassive.

Asher smiled sadly. "She would like that," he said. He looked between them again, wondering whether this was the time. But when would there be a good time to discuss a decades-old affair?

"I know what happened," Asher said quietly.

Emma's eyes darted to her husband, who suddenly looked away from Asher.

"I know because my mother told me," Asher said gently. "At the charity event, she saw the way I looked at Abi. She knew something was going on—I don't know how I ever got anything past her," he continued, and Emma gave a small smile.

"I'm not dismissing the pain it has caused both our families—and, likely, the shame," Asher said, keeping his voice neutral, void of judgment.

William Bennett's face was no longer impassive. It tightened like he was in pain.

Asher returned his attention to Emma. "The morning after the charity event I had a conversation with my father. Mother had obviously told him about Abi and my involvement in IFRT. I made a deal with my father that morning," Asher said, and William looked back to him. "The deal was that I wouldn't further my involvement in IFRT, but they could keep the border permissions I'd set in place. In return, he would publicly support my relationship with Abi."

William's jaw all but fell to the floor. "What else did you offer him in return?"

Asher cleared his throat. "That I would strengthen our ties with your family. That we would show Santina we were prepared to do anything—including burying old feuds—to help Santina prosper. I said I would negotiate with you to build initiatives and additional funding for Santina."

Williams' eyes narrowed. "That's an interesting deal to make without my consent."

Asher held his gaze. "It was, and now I'm asking for you to help me uphold my part of the deal. My father may be dead, but I gave him my word, and I don't intend to back down from it."

William searched his eyes, much like he had when he'd first seen Asher at the charity event. No one said anything, but when Asher saw Emma's pleading eyes lift to her husband, he knew it was a done deal.

"Okay—but I won't be dictated to. I decide the initiatives to spend my money on," William said.

"Thank you," Asher said with a nod. "One more thing . . ." he started, but the words lodged in his throat. "Please tell Abi what happened. My relationship with her was brief, and I don't know where it stands anymore. But if we have a chance, she needs to know the truth, because I won't lie to her about my conversation with my father—and that's a somewhat impossible story to tell without talking about my mother and the reason for the feud. I think your daughter will have the exact same reaction I had when my mother told me."

"And what was that?" William asked, his words clipped.

"Forgiveness. People make mistakes, and from what I can tell, given that your wife is sitting beside you, you haven't repeated the mistake, and you've spent your life making it up to your family."

William rolled his lips over one another and he looked away, his eyes pained. Asher let it go—for now.

Their phones sounded at the same time.

Jesse: ETA 2 minutes.

"They're almost here," Asher said, his voice a whisper. He could barely believe it. Abi was taken a few days ago, but it felt like she'd been gone for months. His entire life had changed, and there was so much they needed to talk about.

The two minutes passed like two years. Asher's foot tapped silently and Emma's eyes never left the doorway. They didn't speak a word, but the silence seemed to have a heartbeat of its own—or maybe it was their heartbeats echoing through the palace.

Finally Asher heard footsteps and voices. Asher, William, and Emma stood in synchronization, like perfectly orchestrated puppets. As the footsteps grew louder, Emma ran from the room. Asher walked toward the door, his eyes following Emma. She neared the end of the hallway when Jesse and Abi, flanked by Rachel and Daniel, rounded the corner.

"Abi!' Emma said, her voice hoarse.

She wrapped her arms around her daughter, but her daughter hissed.

Emma jolted back like she'd touched an electric fence.

"It's okay," Abi said, reaching her hand out for her mother. "It's okay. My back is missing a little skin, that's all. I fell from a rooftop."

Once again Abi was comforting someone else in a moment of her own pain, Asher thought.

Emma cupped her daughter's cheeks as her body began to rock with her tears. Asher stood back, giving them a moment, even though all he wanted to do was hold her in his arms.

Abi's lip was cut and her face painted with yellow and purple bruises. Dark shadows lined her eyes and her hair was tangled and messy, even though it had been pulled up into a bun. Despite it all, she'd never looked more beautiful.

It took Asher a minute to realize William Bennett was right beside him. "We'll work together," William said under his breath. "And I'll tell Abi what happened. But don't *ever* make my mistake, Asher," he said, almost as if he were speaking to his own son. Asher wasn't entirely sure if it was advice or a warning.

"I won't. I give you my word," Asher said as Abi raised her eyes to his.

Jesse moved in. "Abi needs to sit down."

Abi's eyes didn't leave Asher. Ignoring Jesse, Asher moved toward her, drawn like a moth to a flame. He was scared to touch her—to hurt her—but he lifted her chin and guided his lips to hers. Out of respect for her parents, who in this moment he barely remembered were there, he held back from kissing her the way he wanted, but his lips pressed hard against the corner of her mouth that wasn't cut and bloodied. His kiss told her everything he couldn't say in that moment. He didn't know what she'd been through, but he wanted her to know it didn't matter—he wanted her regardless.

Their region had an appalling association with rape. Female rape victims were disowned by their families and outcast like they'd committed the crime themselves instead of being treated with the compassion that should be given to victims. Asher knew it was one of IFRT's greatest struggles in re-homing their rescues, and even though it killed him to think that Abi had endured that, he needed her to know he would love her anyway.

He pulled back, running a thumb over the fresh tears running down her cheek. He wiped them away.

"She needs to sit down," Jesse repeated more firmly.

This time, Asher nodded. Daniel stepped aside and Asher and Rachel helped Abi to the sitting room chairs.

Abi sat on the edge of the chair and as she did, the blanket slipped from her shoulders.

Asher gasped at seeing Abi's light blue T-shirt painted red and stuck to her back. "Why didn't you put a fresh bandage on her back?" he asked, turning to Jesse. He didn't mean for the words to come out as an accusation, but the sight had taken him aback.

"They are fresh," he said, draping the blanket back over her shoulders. "The doctor is here and he'll see Abi in a few minutes. He'll dress the wounds again."

Asher took a calming breath. The last thing Abi needed was him losing it, but his emotions were as raw as her back appeared to be.

William Bennett took a seat beside Abi. "When you were six months old, I said to your mom, 'This kid is going to give me a heart attack.'" William smiled and Abi chuckled. "You scared the hell out of me, Abi. We have a few things to talk about," he said, then added, "in due course," which Asher was sure was directed toward him.

"Like my *administrative* role in IFRT?" she asked, sheepishly.

William's eyebrows lifted. "Yes, that, and other things—but I've never been happier to see you. I love you, kid," he said, kissing her forehead.

"I love you too," Abi said, closing her eyes for a moment.

Asher noticed a lone figure standing by the doorway, shifting uncomfortably. Her eyes were darting around the room, and Asher supposed she'd never seen luxury like this in her life. He guessed this young girl had to be the person who had helped Abi.

Asher gave Abi another moment with her parents and moved toward the girl. "Hello. What is your name?" Asher asked gently.

The girl's big eyes looked at him but it took her a moment to answer. "Lenna," she said, sounding unsure.

Asher smiled. "Thank you, Lenna. You saved Abi's life and we'll take care of you. Whatever you need, you just ask, okay?"

"Okay. Abi need doctor," she said.

Asher paused, noting that she was thinking of Abi first when she likely needed medical attention too. Asher couldn't see any physical wounds, but that didn't mean they weren't hiding beneath her clothes. Her voice sounded much younger than her appearance seemed to indicate, which confused Asher. Maybe she was younger than he'd initially thought. Regardless, she was definitely much too young to have seen the horrors he guessed she'd witnessed.

Movement behind Lenna distracted Asher, and he saw Alistair walking toward him. Alistair looked over the room then continued forward. He didn't stop to greet them; he didn't utter a word. Asher was glad he'd kept walking.

A security team was behind Alistair and they nodded to Asher as they passed. The security team was there under the pretense they were providing security, but Asher now knew they were there to watch his brother as much as anything.

Asher pushed those thoughts from his mind as the doctor entered the room.

"King Asher," he said with a bow.

"Evening," Asher said. "Your patient is ready." He gestured toward the couch.

The doctor kneeled in front of Abi. "I'd like to take you to another room so I can assess your injuries. Would you like someone to go with you?"

"No, I'm fine. Thank you," Abi said, making a move to stand. Her father caught her arm, helping her up, and Asher moved to her other side. He wanted to be by her side, wherever she went, including in the doctor's room.

Security followed as they helped Abi into one of the closest living quarters and sat her on the edge of the bed. William Bennett excused himself, but Asher remained standing.

"Are you sure you're okay? I'll stay with you," Asher said, chewing on his cheek.

Abi gave his hand a squeeze. "I'm okay. Give me a few minutes with the doctor."

He didn't want to leave, but he wasn't going to make this any harder for her. She'd been through hell, and he would be whatever she needed him to be. This wasn't about him.

Reluctantly, he left the room. Jesse was waiting outside with the Bennetts.

"Rachel and Daniel are going to stay tonight at least. They're setting up rooms in one of the guest suites. Lenna will stay with them."

"Who is at the hospital?" Asher asked, torn. He needed to be with Abi, but he hated the thought of his mother being alone.

"Her aide is sitting beside her. She's offered to stay the night," Jesse said.

Asher nodded. His mother and Amelia—her long-standing aide—were good friends. Amelia had been part of their family for as long as he could remember. As a child, Asher had thought it hilarious that his mother's name was Emilia, and her servant's was Amelia; now, he was just grateful she was there for her.

"Asher, I'd like to offer to stay with her tonight. Amelia could come in the morning and that way you'll have some time with Abi," Emma said.

"Thank you," Asher said, knowing that would make his mother happy. "There's a security team with her, but I don't want her to feel alone." His mother wasn't weak, but Asher wanted her to have people speak to her, all the same, to tell her how much she was loved and that she needed to wake up.

He wanted to tell her to keep fighting, because he needed her.

Santina needed her.

Emma held her gaze on him, looking torn. Eventually she spoke the words she'd so clearly been wrestling with in her mind. "You have the best qualities of your mother, and the best of your father. I don't envy you—the title you bear—but I told my family after I saw your coronation ceremony that you should be king. Your father made a good decision."

Asher didn't know what to say. He mustered, "Thank you," but it seemed totally inadequate.

Jesse stepped in to save him. "I'll arrange an escort for you when you're ready to leave," he said to Emma, and then he turned to Asher. "May I please have a few minutes?"

Asher nodded. "Excuse me," he said to the Bennetts before following Jesse.

ASHER

*A*sher followed Jesse into the king's office.
His office.

He sat in the chair behind the desk, and he'd never felt more out of place.

"I have a video call scheduled for us in a few minutes," Jesse said. "I know Luke provided a few details to you, but I want you to meet the team. I don't know them personally, but I know of them—everyone in the security world does. They don't take on new clients anymore, but given that they're an international firm with clients all over the world, keeping Santina stable is of interest to them. My cousin, Vincent, knows them and has vouched for them. Vincent is a man of . . . ruthless character. He sets rules and the world obeys, because they know the consequences if they don't. He has known this team for years, and Vincent hears things other don't. He says we can trust them."

Asher searched Jesse's eyes. "Trust . . . That's the funny thing—right now I don't know who to trust."

Jesse nodded. "I understand, and that's exactly why I think this team should be brought in. They have no personal stake in the politics of our region and have nothing to gain from seeing Santina fall."

Asher didn't know what to do. "I'll speak with them and then decide," he said eventually.

"Good," Jesse said, dragging a chair to sit beside Asher as he turned on the television screen mounted on the wall opposite the desk.

Asher looked at the growing stack of mail. It was like two towers threatening to topple over. He needed to work, needed to get back to routine—and tomorrow he would.

Now that Abi was home and his mother was stable, life was as good as it was going to get, for a little while at least. It was time to stop feeling sorry for himself.

Santina needed him.

The television screen flickered and five faces looked at him.

Compelling black eyes drew him in. "Your Majesty, I'm James Thomas. This is my brother, Deacon. And this is Samuel, Jarrod, and Cami."

"Hello," Asher said, his voice masking the well of emotions that were threatening to swallow him. "Thank you for meeting with us."

"Firstly," Deacon said, "our condolences for Noah and your father."

Asher nodded. He was scared to think about them, because if he did, he might break down.

"We operate Thomas Security," Deacon continued. "We're based in New York but have clients and thus agents all over the world. We specialize in cases that require multiple layers of security. Jesse contacted us after your father's death, and we've done a preliminary assessment of your security and looked at a few key pieces of intelligence surrounding your father's passing," he said. "We understand the enormous pressure you're under right now, but regardless of whether we work together in the future or not, we want to give you this advice: Your enemies are watching, and right now you need to show them you're strong and not afraid. Your speech on the balcony was perfect. Every time you're in public or on the telephone, that's the person you need to be—no matter how hard it is."

James Thomas nodded. "The best thing you can do is to confuse whoever is behind these attacks. You want to keep them guessing about your next move so they can't counter it. People are predictable when they're afraid, and your enemies will use that to their advantage."

"But *who* are my enemies?" Asher asked, his voice strained.

The man introduced as Samuel cleared his throat. "We're still working on that, but so far we have narrowed the list down to twenty key players."

Asher raised an eyebrow. "From Adani?" he asked.

"From Adani," James said with a nod, "and some local."

Asher met James's gaze. "Did Alistair make that list?"

"Alistair made the list," James said, his eyes seeming to search Asher's. James continued, "I've been where you are—when you don't know who to trust—and I'm sorry you're in this position. I understand you might not want to face the fact that Alistair is involved, but we have questions for him, and you might not like his answers."

Asher looked at them all. "I want the answers, and I want everyone involved to be punished. I won't be lenient on anyone—family or not—who has been involved in Noah's murder, the attack on my parents, or Abi's kidnapping. No one will be spared."

James gave a nod that indicated he approved of Asher's answer. "Good—then we'll work well together. That said, Abi's case is slightly more complex than investigating the death of Noah or the attack on your parents," James said, seeming to choose his words carefully.

"It will be best if we consult directly with Jesse on Abi's case," James said.

Asher raised an eyebrow. "Why is that?"

"For the same reason my wife doesn't know all the details of my past," James said, his face remaining impassive. "I suspect Abi has a criminal record—however good her intentions—that it will not serve you to know. It will put you in a position of conflict given your title, and if you're ever questioned over her past, it will be best if you can be honest and say you don't know. If something arises that we think you do need to know, Jesse and I will make that decision."

Asher looked to Jesse, who nodded, indicating he was onboard with this plan.

"Can you find the information you need to investigate the murders and the kidnapping? Won't you need teams here in Santina?" Asher asked.

James nodded. "We have methods of obtaining information that others don't have, we have skill sets that others don't have, and we can find information that government agencies pay us a lot of money for. If you're asking out of concern for Abi's criminal past being exposed—assuming there is one—I can assure you that if we find the information, we will make sure it's buried so deep that no one will ever see it. Given your title, you should work with us purely for this reason, even if we don't investigate the murders."

"The problem is: how do I know whether or not I can trust you?" Asher asked cautiously.

"You can't know that," Deacon said flatly. "Not right now. Like all relationships, trust takes time. But whether you hire us or not, if we wanted to find the information, we could. If we wanted to expose it, we could. We have no desire to do that, and we wouldn't waste our resources on such an activity when we have nothing to gain. If you ask anyone in the industry about Thomas Security, they'll tell you we're the people who are called when someone's world starts to crumble."

"You're under enormous pressure right now," James continued. "A good security strategy will mean you can focus on Santina and fulfilling your role, and you won't have to think about watching your back."

Asher nodded, his eyes dropping to his towering stacks of mail. He needed to be able to focus on his job. He needed that more than anything.

He looked back to the screen.

"What is this going to cost?" Asher asked.

"That will depend on the strategy we devise. Vincent, at Jesse's request, has asked this of us as a favor," James said with a slight smile, "and I like having a man like Vincent owe me something. But there will be some additional costs involved."

"I can't make this decision without knowing what those costs are," Asher said. "Santina is not a rich kingdom."

James Thomas looked him dead in the eyes. "You might be richer than you think."

Asher's eyebrows wove together. "How do you mean? We can barely feed our people."

"We are still looking into this, so I'm hesitant to give you full details at this stage, but it seems as if Alistair became aware of a potential oil reserve. We're verifying this data, but if our initial intelligence is correct, the reserve sits below the holy ruins at Lithe. It is one of the few sites that had never been excavated, for obvious reasons. Your father discovered Alistair's extracurricular activities two days before his death."

"He said nothing of this to me," Asher said slowly. *Why wouldn't he have told me?*

"I think that's because he didn't get a chance," James broke in. "He ordered his own testing to be done, and they started work the day he was killed. The men who were performing the testing haven't been seen since, and the company is refusing to talk."

"What do you mean by 'haven't been seen since'?" Asher asked. "Are they dead? Or missing?"

"Likely dead," James said without pause. "But we would need to send a team to the site to investigate that. Everything we've done so far has been performed remotely, but if you want us to work with you, the sooner we get a full team to Santina the better."

"And who would be on this team?" Asher asked. "Will you be coming to Santina?"

"No," James said. "I will send multiple teams to perform various roles. If I turn up in Santina unexpectedly, you'll know things are really bad."

"How much worse can things get?" Asher asked, the strain of the last few days taking its toll. "My father is dead. Noah is dead. My mother is fighting for her life, and Abi only just made it home alive." His eyes narrowed at James Thomas's surprisingly calm expression.

"Things can always get worse," James said. "You don't have to hire us, Your Majesty—"

Asher waved his hand. "Call me Asher, please," he said.

James nodded. "You don't have to hire us, Asher, but you do need to hire someone. You need a team that doesn't have an interest in Santina or the region. Jesse can't do this alone—his security team isn't big enough. You need multiple teams, Abi needs multiple teams, your mother needs multiple teams, and you need at least four teams to follow Alistair and investigate the other names on our list. This is a huge operation now, and I don't say this to frighten you—you already know it—but you're next on the list. Maybe your enemies will wait for Santina to fall, but maybe they'll get impatient and decide to *make* it fall. They tried to strip everything from you, Asher, and they won't hesitate to tidy up loose ends. Once that's done, you're next. And if that happens, Santina *will* fall."

Asher looked away, his jaw grinding. His gaze landed on a photo of his parents—their wedding photo. He would not fail them.

"Okay," Asher said. "What happens first?"

James nodded his approval. "First we install a security system that will ensure there's not a blind spot in the entire palace. I have a team on standby—they landed a few hours ago. I didn't want to be presumptive, but the faster we move, the greater our chance of keeping you alive. The team will work overnight installing the cameras, and tomorrow they'll be in the ceiling to finish the wiring. I want to do it tonight while Alistair is asleep. The less he knows, the better."

"Alistair sleeps during the day," Asher said. *And parties all night.*

James smirked. "Not tonight. He's fast asleep, and he won't be waking up anytime soon."

Asher frowned. Had Alistair drunk too much and passed out?

"Get some sleep," Deacon said. "We'll handle things. We've got you covered, and we'll provide an update and strategy briefing in the morning."

"Thank you," Asher said before the screen went blank.

He turned to Jesse. "What's with Alistair? How much has he been drinking?" Asher hadn't seen him drink at the hospital, but maybe he had been busy making up for that temporary sobriety.

Jesse gave an odd grin. "He only had one drink—the one I gave him. I drugged him at James Thomas's request."

ABI

Abi sucked in a breath as new bandages were applied to her back.

"That's it, you're done for this evening," the doctor said with gentle eyes. "I'll give you some pain relief. Take some before bed and again when you wake up. I'll be back tomorrow morning to see how you're doing."

He pulled a little white bottle from his bag and handed it to her.

"Keep ice on your ankle and we'll X-ray it tomorrow, but it's likely just a slight sprain," he said.

"Thank you," Abi said, and he gave a gentle nod before excusing himself.

In the silence of the room, Abi took her first good look at her surroundings. She was in a suite of some kind—she supposed it was guest quarters. The room was much more minimal than she'd expected. It was void of luxurious velvet and detailed ceilings. It was a far cry from the sitting room she'd first been taken into, but it was more elegant. The gray and beige color schemes matched those of her own apartment, which was an odd coincidence.

A knock at the door stole her attention and she called out, "Come in."

Asher entered, closing the door behind him, and she was glad to finally have a moment alone with him.

Their eyes met and her chest warmed.

"Hey," Abi said, her voice much higher than usual.

The corner of Asher's lips turned up. "Hey," he said, taking his suit jacket off and slinging it over another chair. "Your parents have gone. They'll be back in the morning. Rachel, Lenna, and Daniel are settled in the guest rooms."

"Thank you," Abi said, tucking a loose strand behind her ear. She desperately wanted a hot shower, but the doctor had said she couldn't because of her back.

"It's the least I could do," Asher said, taking a seat beside her. He cupped her cheeks in his hands and Abi closed her eyes, falling into a kiss she'd thought she'd never get again.

"Talk to me," Asher said, his voice low. "Tell me everything that happened, Abi."

She opened her eyes, meeting his with a sigh. "I don't even know where to start," she said, resting her elbow on the top of the couch, supporting her back.

Asher threaded his fingers through hers and brought them to his lips. "I need to know. Start at the beginning. I have all night, and I'm not going anywhere."

"Okay, but do you have wine? I'd really love a glass of red," she said with a cheeky grin.

"I'll be back in a minute," Asher said before placing a kiss on her cheek.

Abi sat staring at the walls, wondering if she should turn the television on. She looked for the remote control and saw it was across the room—too much effort, she decided.

Asher came back with a bottle and two glasses. Abi recognized the label. "You really liked it," she said with a small smile. It was the same bottle she'd bought the night he'd come to their apartment, before they'd gone to the ruins. She'd thought things were complicated then but she'd had no idea of just how complicated they would become.

Asher grinned. "I did. Shame about the price tag. I spent my entire monthly allowance on the one bottle."

Abi grinned. "Nothing but the best for the Prin—"

Her eyes widened slightly as she stopped herself. *King.* He was King, by the most horrific circumstances, and Abi knew he didn't want the title.

"King," he said, his voice sounding strained, and then he gave a forced smile. "Wine. Then tell me what happened, and then I'll tell you everything you missed."

"Deal," Abi said quietly, taking the glass from his hands and settling in. "A car passed me on the highway and straight away I sensed something wasn't right, but the car passed me and continued on, so I told myself I was overreacting. When I saw the car pulled up on the side of the road a few minutes later, I knew I'd been right. A man was standing outside the car holding a gun, and I knew what was going to happen. They fired at my car, forcing me off the road. At that point I had two options: run and be shot at, or stop and be taken. I stopped, because I knew that was the surest way of surviving. If I'd tried to run, they would've killed me the second I stepped outside the car."

She continued on and told him everything she could remember. Some details were clear, others were muddled. Trauma did that, she knew.

"Is that all?" Asher asked, his eyes searching hers.

She tilted her head to the side. "Yes. What do you think I left out?"

Asher chewed on his cheek. "I'm not saying you left anything out, but I want you to be able to tell me everything. I know what happens to captive women, Abi, and if it happened, it's okay. I'm still here for you, I still want you—more than I ever have."

"If they raped me, you mean?" Abi asked, her voice even and calm. She knew these were hard subjects, but given her line of work, she'd been talking about them for years, and that made it slightly easier.

"Yes. I know you told Jesse you weren't, but he wondered if you didn't tell him because that's a hard thing to tell a stranger. I want you to be able to tell me, if you need to," Asher said, his eyes caressing her.

Abi dragged her bottom lip through her teeth. "The irony of it all is that Lamberi was my saving grace. Because I was being prepared for him, he didn't want the men to have their way with me. Did they touch me? Yes—they removed my clothing, they searched my cavities—which was really just an excuse for them to touch me. But did they force themselves on me for intercourse? No, by some miracle they didn't," she said, her voice a hoarse whisper. "It didn't happen."

"I believe you," he said, running his thumb over her knuckles.

"But what if it had?" Abi asked, watching him carefully.

Asher didn't hesitate to respond. "Then I would find you the best therapist in Santina—in the world—and I would do everything I could to help you work through it."

She smiled. He was a good man, her King. "Now it's your turn," she said.

He put his empty glass down and she noticed that he refilled hers, but not his own. When Asher began to talk, she had no idea of the things she would hear. So much tragedy, too much for anyone's heart, but amongst it all there was an ember of hope.

"You fought for us," Abi said. It wasn't a question. He'd made a deal with King Martin. "But I still don't really understand."

"Your parents are going to explain that side of things. It's not my story to tell," he said gently.

Abi frowned, but didn't want to push it. She focused on the positive. "Your father was really going to support our relationship?"

Asher nodded. "I want you. I've wanted you since the moment I walked into IFRT," he said with heated eyes. "I'm not asking you to marry me right now, but my father was right: who I choose to be my queen will be one of the biggest decisions I'll ever make. I look at my parents and know there is no way my father could've been the king he was without my mother's support."

He gently squeezed her hand. "So this is where we are now, Abi. If this is not a life you want—and I fully understand why it wouldn't be—you have the option to walk away. I don't. As much as I don't know if I'm prepared for this role, or if I can even lead Santina, my father made this decision with full confidence and to abdicate would be to dishonor him. I won't do it."

Abi smiled sadly. She loved the determination in his voice, and she knew he could lead Santina, even if he didn't—but there were other things to consider. "Asher, even if I wanted to, there are so many concerns with me being Queen: my past, for one, not to mention a possible fallout with Lamberi. I don't want to bring you more harm. I am the worst person to consider for the role," Abi said as tears stung her eyes. She looked away. She'd considered these things from the moment she'd heard he was King, but only now did the realization set in. She would need to let him go.

"Those are all the reasons to not, but what about the reasons to?" Asher asked. "Abi, look at me. You're brave, far braver than anyone I know. You're compassionate, you're caring, and—equally important for the role—you can handle pressure. All those reasons are far more important than the others. A falling out with Lamberi is possible, if not likely, regardless of our relationship," Asher paused. "I won't back down to Adani, Abi. They don't get away with murdering Noah and my father, attempting to murder my mother, and kidnapping you. Not while I'm King."

She didn't respond, she couldn't find the right words. She wanted him, too—she had since the moment they'd met—but she didn't know how to be Queen. She didn't know what would happen to IFRT, either, but that was a separate issue, because with her identity exposed in Adani, there were serious concerns and issues with her remaining as the leader anyway.

"If you want to help people—to serve—the role of queen will help you reach more than you'll ever be able to help through IFRT. I need someone strong, Abi. And I want you," he said.

Abi met his tortured eyes. It wasn't a plea, but she knew he meant every word. Asher could do it alone, but he didn't want to.

"Where do we even start?" she asked, suddenly feeling faint.

Asher gave her an odd look. "I have no fucking idea," he said with a strained laugh.

Abi didn't know if it was the wine going to her head or pure exhaustion, but she laughed heartily.

"One day at a time," he said with a beautiful smile. "Or so that's what everyone keeps telling me. I'm not asking for a forever commitment right now. I'm just asking you to give us a chance. Hell, we might not work out. You might get a few months into this and decide it isn't what you want. And that's fine—but please give us a chance. The first proper chance we've had."

Asher's eyes were like deep wells, pulling her in, and she was drowning in them.

ASHER

His heart refused to beat as he waited patiently for her response. Abi nodded and a smile spread across her lips. "Let's give us a chance," she said.

Asher leaned in and pressed his lips against hers. He'd never needed her more. Her lips parted and his tongue swept over hers. She tasted like wine—his favorite wine. His body burned for her, but he didn't know how to hold her without hurting her. His lips trailed down her neck, but she pulled back when he reached her collarbone.

"What's wrong?" he asked quickly.

"Nothing," she said, then scrunched up her nose. "I'd just rather have a shower before you kiss me any more. There's only so much face wipes can do," she said, shaking her head and looking away.

"Hey," he said, turning her face back to him. "I'll help you with the shower. Or I can get someone to do that," he added quickly.

Abi waved her hand dismissively. "Just help me into the bathroom and give me ten minutes and I'll be good. I'd rather not have anyone with me."

He kissed her forehead. "Okay." He grabbed the crutches that had been left standing against the living room wall and then helped her up. He would've carried her, but he wasn't sure he could lift her without hurting her back.

Asher walked beside her as she hobbled into the bathroom. He dragged a chair in and positioned it next to the vanity, then found some clean towels and soap. "What else do you need?"

"A razor and something to sleep in," she said.

"Easily done, give me a second," he said, making sure she was sitting and comfortable before he left.

He strode toward his living quarters and found a T-shirt and boxers for her to wear, and then he grabbed a new razor from his bathroom. Security was watching him and followed him back to the guest quarters.

He closed the bathroom door behind him, giving them some privacy. "Anything else?" he asked.

She smiled. "No, all good. You can leave now," she said.

Asher chuckled. "I get the hint. I'll be right outside; yell out if you need anything," he said before closing the door.

Asher refilled Abi's glass and placed it beside the bed. He took his empty glass to the kitchen sink. He turned on the television in the bedroom and looked through the movies, but he muted the sound—he wanted to be able to hear Abi if she needed something.

He checked his watch and settled on the end of the bed, catching the end of a movie he'd seen many times, but he was barely watching it at all. His mind wandered, trying to visualize everything she had been through—and when his blood began to boil, he checked his phone. There was nothing from Jesse, and that was good news, he supposed.

Eventually, the bathroom door opened and Abi appeared, dressed in his T-shirt and boxers. Asher went to her, but she was handling the crutches like a pro.

"I'm actually pretty good at these things," she said with a wry smile. "I sprained my ankle in high school and I was on crutches for a month, I think."

And true to her word, she sped right past him.

"Are you tired?" Asher asked.

"Yeah," she said, then looked pained. "I don't know if I'll sleep, though."

Asher gave a sad smile. "That makes two of us. Let's watch a movie."

He helped her into bed, fighting to keep his anger under control as she winced before settling on her side, facing the middle of the bed. Asher stripped down to his boxers and slid in next to her. He wasn't leaving her—not tonight. He needed to know she was safe.

"Come closer," she whispered with heated eyes.

He moved into the center and she laid her cheek on his chest, rolling into him. Her leg slipped between his.

He took her hand, threading their fingers together.

"Comfortable?" he asked, kissing the crown of her head.

"Yes," she said lazily. She placed a kiss on his bare chest.

She was home.

In his arms.

And he was never letting her go.

* * *

Asher awoke to the sound of Abi's voice. She shifted restlessly beside him.

"Don't touch me," she said angrily, and Asher's eyes snapped open.

He abruptly leaned away before he realized she was dreaming. Her words were mumbled, and through the light cast from the television, he could see her eyelids fluttering violently.

"Don't touch me," she repeated with more venom in her voice. Her knee slammed into his and Asher winced.

He didn't know whether to wake her or let the dream pass—but he didn't get the chance to make the decision.

Her fist flew at him as she screamed, "Don't touch me!"

Her fist connected with the base of his throat, her knuckles crunching against his collarbone.

The air was knocked from Asher's lungs, and he scrambled out of bed just as Jesse burst through the door with his weapon raised.

"What's going on?" Jesse demanded, looking between them with wide eyes.

Asher was wheezing in a breath, desperately trying to fill his lungs with air. His hand went to his throat.

Abi's eyes opened and were filled with panic. She looked from Jesse to Asher, back to Jesse.

"Ash?" Jesse ran to his side. "Breathe," he said, before shouting, "Get the doctor!"

Jesse looked to Abi. "What happened?" he growled.

Asher held up a hand, trying to slow down the situation but he was too out of breath to speak. Air seemed to be leaking from his throat but nothing was going back in.

"Give me . . . a . . . second," Asher wheezed.

Asher massaged his neck, an instinctive move as he tried to relax his muscles. The walls shifted and he must've swayed because Jesse grabbed his arm, sitting him on the edge of the bed.

"What's wrong with him?" Abi asked hurriedly. She was clearly awake now, but Asher didn't have the breath to explain it to anyone. She crawled across the bed but Jesse put his hand up, stopping her.

Slowly, air began to fill his lungs and he no longer felt like he was suffocating. He leaned forward, resting his elbows on his knees, sucking in deep breaths. The doctor rushed in, but Asher shot Jesse a pleading look, shaking his head.

"It's okay, I can breathe," Asher said.

Jesse's eyebrows wove together. He looked between Asher and Abi again.

"Give me a minute," Asher said, drawing a long breath, settling the adrenaline racing through his veins. He cleared his throat and drank a little water. It went down his throat, so he assumed no major damage had been done.

"Ash," Jesse said, his voice a warning.

"A minute," Asher repeated firmly.

"One minute," Jesse said with narrowed eyes before leaving.

When the door closed, Asher turned to an alarmed Abi.

"What happened?" she asked, her voice a hoarse whisper.

Asher wanted to tread carefully, but he couldn't explain what had happened without telling her the truth.

"You were dreaming," he said.

The corner of her eyes creased and then her cheeks flushed. Was she embarrassed?

"Was I talking?" she asked tentatively.

"You said, 'Don't touch me.'"

Her eyes widened and then narrowed, like she was searching through her memories.

She shook her head. "I keep waking up feeling like I've been dreaming, but I can't remember the dream. It started in the cells," she said. She paused, and he saw the realization hit her. "Did you try and wake me?"

"No. I was contemplating whether I should do that, and then . . ." He didn't want to tell her the truth, didn't want to cause her any more pain.

"Did I strangle . . . ?" Her voice trailed off.

Asher mustered a small smile. "No," he said, shaking his head. "But you throw a nice punch."

Her jaw fell open. "I punched you?" she asked, bending over like he'd just done the same to her. "In the throat?" She made a noise that sounded like a cry. "I could've killed you! I can't be here, I shouldn't be here," she whispered in a rush, then moved, clearly forgetting about her ankle in the chaos of what had just happened.

She stood, hissing as she grabbed the bedside table. Asher rushed toward her.

"Stop, please. I'm okay," he said with a rough voice, even though the air had returned to his lungs.

But Abi wouldn't hear it. "I'm sorry, I'm so sorry. Let me go," she said, but Asher refused to release his grip.

"Don't go. Please don't," Asher begged. "I haven't slept properly since

Noah died. I've heard nothing but your screaming echoing through the hallways since you were taken. Tonight was the first slice of peace I've had in weeks. Don't leave me tonight. I'll move to the edge of the bed, far away from your hands—but please don't go." He was begging and he meant every word. He knew she was right—if her fist had landed an inch higher she could've killed him—but he still didn't want her to go.

Her eyes looked pained, tormented. "What was I saying?"

"Don't touch me," he repeated hoarsely.

She frowned, and her eyes drifted to the right like she was thinking it through. "I must've been dreaming about Lamberi," she said, her voice sounding far away. "I don't know why I can't see—remember—the dreams."

Asher tucked a strand of hair behind her ear. "I don't know," he admitted. "But you need to speak to someone about what happened. Tomorrow. We'll sort this out then. Right now I just want to sleep."

He noticed the cut on her lip was bleeding. He grabbed a tissue from the bedside table and dabbed it to her lip. Her face scrunched for a second but she didn't push him away.

"I'm so sorry," she whispered.

He kissed her forehead, and his lips lingered. "It's okay, it was a dream. And this might be a good lesson for me to remember when I'm going to do something that will piss you off," he said, trying to make a joke.

She gave a strained laugh. "This is horrible. I'll sleep on the couch where I can be close, but at a safe distance."

"No. That's too far away," he told her quietly.

A knock at the door interrupted them.

Abi groaned. "He already thinks I'm a liar, now he's going to think I'm—"

"He doesn't think you're a liar," Asher said, waving a hand. "Jesse was impressed by the way you handled the situation in Adani, and Jesse's not impressed easily."

"He's hard to read," Abi said.

Another knock on the door.

"Not tonight," Asher said with a thin smile. "I'll speak to him and be back in a few minutes."

Jesse was sitting on the couch with the doctor when Asher entered the living room.

"I'm okay," he said, closing the bedroom door behind him.

"The doctor will confirm that. Please take a seat," Jesse said.

Asher sat on the edge of the coffee table, aware he was dressed in nothing but his boxer shorts. The doctor didn't seem to notice, nor did Jesse.

"She was dreaming and her fist connected with my collarbone, but I think it just caught my throat. I couldn't breathe for a few moments, but I feel fine now," Asher said.

The doctor opened his bag and pulled out a stethoscope. He listened to Asher's breathing and then asked Asher to stick out his tongue so he could look down his throat.

"I want to image it tomorrow, but it seems you were very, very lucky," the doctor said. "If her fist had connected differently, we might not be having this conversation. I'll get you an ice pack to put on your throat to help with bruising. I want you to eat and drink something now so that I can make sure you can get it down and keep it down."

Jesse was up and headed toward the kitchen before the doctor had finished.

He came back with some yogurt and a glass of water. Asher ate and swallowed and felt no pain.

The doctor nodded his approval. "Ice, and then we'll scan it tomorrow just to make sure there's no small tear or anything else I need to be aware of."

"Thank you," Asher said.

"It's my honor, Your Majesty," the doctor said.

Asher had never felt less like a king sitting in his boxer shorts eating yogurt in the middle of the night. It was almost funny—except that he couldn't think about being king without thinking of his father's violent death.

"I'll be back in a few minutes," the doctor said.

"This is a concern, Ash," Jesse said when they were alone. His voice was low and Asher hoped Abi couldn't hear.

"I know. I should've woken her when I heard her talking, but I didn't expect her fists to start flying," Asher said.

"It's post-traumatic stress, which is not surprising at all," Jesse said. "But it's not a good idea to be sleeping in the same bed as her right now. I'm doing everything to keep you alive, and she could've killed you. And then what?" he asked, shaking his head. "How would she live with that, if she'd woken up and realized what she'd done?"

"I'll sleep on the edge of the bed with my back to her. I know the risks—trust me, they were very clear as I was fighting to breathe—but tonight I actually slept. For the first time in weeks, I slept properly," Asher said flatly.

Jesse rubbed the back of his neck. "Okay, but I'm putting a recording device in that room, and if she seems unsettled I'm coming in there and pulling you out of bed."

"Okay," Asher said without pause. "Speaking of recording devices, how is the install going?"

Jesse nodded. "They're on schedule and Alistair is still asleep," Jesse said as he texted someone on his phone.

The doctor returned a few minutes later with two ice packs. "One for you, and a fresh one for Abi's ankle," he said.

"Thank you again," Asher said with a nod. Another security guard entered and passed Jesse a small box.

He pulled out the device, which looked like a pen. He passed it to Asher. "Put it on the bedside table closest to Abi."

Asher took the pen and ice packs and returned the bedroom. Abi's eyes landed on him when he entered and he gave her a smile. "This one is for you," he said, passing her an ice pack. He put the pen on the bedside table. "And that's our safety net. If you start dreaming again, Jesse will come in and wake us before anything can happen."

Her shoulders relaxed.

Asher climbed into bed and pulled the covers up to his waist. He put the ice pack on his throat and turned to Abi. "Look at us," he said with a lopsided grin.

"I'm so sorry," she said. "I can't even promise you it won't happen again."

Asher took her hand, threading his fingers through hers. He noticed several small cuts on them, and that the thick bandages around her wrist were still clean—he was glad she wasn't bleeding through them again.

"It was an accident. And I just want to sleep," Asher said softly, his voice sounding more tired by the second.

Abi didn't respond.

"What's wrong?" Asher asked.

"I'm scared to sleep," she whispered, looking away.

He rolled in to face her and brought her mouth to his. He kissed her, wanting to take her pain away—or at least make her forget it for a moment.

When she kissed him back with a hunger that surprised him, a groan slipped from his throat. He remembered the pen.

"I don't know how sensitive that pen is," Asher whispered. "But perhaps don't say, or moan"—he smirked—"anything you don't want Jesse to hear."

She wiggled her eyebrows and Asher chuckled.

His hand cupped her ass and he drew her in. "Kiss me. Kiss me like you did a few seconds ago. That's how I always want you to kiss me."

Her eyes heated and her lips parted.

Asher closed his eyes, reveling in her kiss. His hand threaded through her hair, tugging her mouth closer. She moaned, and Asher didn't care—it barely registered in his mind.

So much was wrong in the world, but in Abi's arms, he'd always felt like anything was possible.

She shifted, and he put his hands on her hips, guiding her on top of him. He kissed her until he was breathless, and then kissed her harder. He ached for her, and he was well aware she could feel him against her hips. She rocked against him and he bit his lip. He stilled, needing to gain some control.

"As much as I love this," he said, forcing the words out in a rushed whisper, "I'm not sure how much control I have right now, and tonight is not the night. And if you do that again, I may lose this tiny piece of self-control I'm holding onto."

She gave a sultry smirk, then laid her head on the pillow beside him. The soft sigh that slipped from her lips was the most erotic sound he'd ever heard.

COLONEL STEVENS

The colonel held the handwritten letter in his hands. He'd been looking at it all night, and the envelope was addressed and ready.

A letter to King Asher.

A letter of everything he'd seen and felt that wasn't right. A letter he wished he'd written for King Martin.

He looked at the letter one last time, knowing there would be serious implications for the accusations he was making, but the easy thing and the right thing were rarely the same, and they certainly weren't in this case. A poison had leaked into Santina, like carbon monoxide—deadly, yet silent—and while it might already be too late for Santina, King Asher had to know.

Colonel Stevens folded the letter and placed it in the envelope. His life would change once this letter was delivered, and though he didn't know if it would change for the better or worse, he at least knew he was doing the right thing. When he closed his eyes at night, he would be able to live with his decisions.

He thought about King Martin as he sealed the envelope and placed it in his wife's handbag with the mail to be posted tomorrow.

Could Colonel Stevens have saved King Martin's life if he'd spoken up sooner?

He knew that was a question he would never be able to answer; he didn't know if King Martin would've believed his suspicions even if he'd voiced them. Would he have believed that the Kingdom's greatest threat came from one whom King Martin had trusted?

The colonel sighed as he returned to his office and put his diary and pens away in his desk drawer.

His eyes darted to the window when he heard the neighbor's dog barking. The sensor light hadn't been activated, and the colonel's eyes snapped to the computer screen of security footage. He checked each field but he couldn't see any motion.

His ears strained to listen but the house was silent. His wife was asleep upstairs, and his children vacated the nest long ago.

A muffled sound from the back of the house drew his attention. He grabbed his pistol from his desk drawer as his eyes scanned the security footage again. If someone was in his house, he should be able to see them. He'd upgraded his security system only six months ago, and it was the best he could buy.

The colonel inched toward the closed door of his study and paused to listen. He heard nothing. He thought of his wife sleeping upstairs, and he inched the door open silently, carefully.

He paused again. Not a sound. The dog had stopped barking.

Maybe it was nothing.

He wanted to believe that, but he didn't. Something didn't feel right.

He checked the hallway, and when it was clear he darted toward the staircase, taking shelter beneath it as he scoped out the adjoining hallway.

He heard the dog barking again, but his house was silent.

The colonel raised his weapon and inched forward, moving toward the kitchen. Light from the neighbor's outdoor security lights filtered through the kitchen windows.

His eyes went to the door. It was closed, and the lock didn't appear tampered with, but without fully inspecting it he couldn't be sure. He looked down and saw a partial footprint.

He stilled.

His wife had washed the floors after dinner, and he hadn't been outside since.

He spun around, his weapon raised, his finger steady on the trigger. He inched back toward the staircase, fearing the intruder would think he was asleep upstairs where his wife was sleeping.

He took one step toward the staircase when four figures emerged from the darkness. His finger pulled the trigger, but he didn't get a chance to find out if he'd shot any of the intruders.

His world went black.

* * *

THE COLONEL AWOKE to a hand connecting to the side of his face. His skin stung and his head throbbed, but that was the least of his concerns as he took in the nightmare he'd woken up in.

Cold metal pressed against the back of his head, and he knew if he made one wrong move, the man holding the pistol to his head would pull the trigger.

He quickly counted the men—four—and ascertained he hadn't shot anyone. His eyes darted around the room he was being held in. White walls, stained gray carpet. He had no idea where he was, but he wasn't in his home.

A lamp in the corner provided the only light and the colonel noted the drab curtains covering the windows. He assumed it was still night and that he'd only been out for a few minutes, but he had no way of knowing that in this dungeon.

He forced himself to think through the pain. It didn't matter where he was; it only mattered that he escaped. That was his focus. He assessed the size of the men and in the limited light, counted the number of weapons he could see.

"You're wasting our time," a low voice said from behind him. The man was a Santinian—the colonel was sure of it.

The colonel didn't respond. He knew the less he spoke the better. He shifted his wrists, not surprised to find they were bound together. He did the same with his feet, but his ankles were bound—likely to the legs of the chair he was sitting on.

The man in front of him spoke. "You're going to cooperate with us, Colonel, otherwise your wife will find her neck underneath my knife."

The colonel's stomach churned violently. Had they taken her too? Or was she home in bed? Had his gun actually fired? He couldn't remember.

The man smirked as he watched the colonel trying to piece it all together. "You've been asking lots of questions, Colonel. Questions you don't need the answers to," the same man said.

The colonel didn't recognize his voice.

"I am a servant of Santina," the colonel said, his voice steady. "It is my job to ask questions regarding the security of our Kingdom." His fear had morphed into anger—he would fight, because his wife needed him. There was a chance they had already killed her, but the colonel doubted they were that stupid. If she was dead, there wasn't a chance he'd speak.

"You overstepped your boundary, Colonel. You assisted a murderer," he said.

The colonel raised his eyebrows. "I did no such thing," he said through gritted teeth.

"Really? Is Abigail Bennett not a murderer?" a different figure asked, emerging from the dark corner of the room.

The colonel stilled. He hadn't seen him there. How many more were there? The questions ran through his mind like a wildfire and his hopes of escaping went up in flames.

"I don't know anything about Abigail Bennett. I gave her border permissions—that's it," the Colonel said.

"So you didn't see her murder multiple men on the highway to Santina?"

The colonel frowned. "I don't know what you're talking about."

The corner of the man's lips turned up. "Really? She dropped her weapon for you, though, didn't she, Colonel? She trusted you and dropped her weapon. You kicked it aside and one of your men picked it up."

The colonel's mind raced as he recalled memories from that night. Everything that had just been spoken was true. Had someone talked? Or had someone else been there, watching them?

"I can see you trying to figure it out," the man continued. "Let me help you: there was another car behind them, one driving with its lights off. They saw and recorded everything, and when Abigail Bennett becomes queen, the world will see it."

"They will see a person acting in self-defense," the colonel said tightly.

The man smirked. "Call it what you like. The people will see what we show them."

"So you're going to blackmail the king?" the colonel asked through gritted teeth.

"We're not blackmailing anyone. I'm just telling you what's going to happen because you won't be here to see it. You refused to join the Revolt, and this is the consequence. Who have you spoken to regarding your security concerns, Colonel?"

"No one," the colonel answered without hesitation. No one, because the letter was still in his wife's handbag.

"I don't believe you, and you have ten seconds to convince me you're not lying," the man said with a haunting grin.

"I haven't spoken to a soul—" The colonel hissed in a violent breath and screamed, his hands feeling like they were on fire.

The man in front of him smirked again, but the colonel didn't see it.

All he could do was rock in agony.

ABI

Her eyelids fluttered, but she forced her eyes to stay closed. She focused on the scent of his cologne as her fingers traced his rippled abdomen, listened to his breathing as it calmed to a slow and steady pace.

Abi willed her mind to be quiet, but she couldn't stop thinking about how they'd gotten there. Within days, their lives as they'd known them had been shattered, and they were left with a few pieces to pick up again. What would become of them? What would become of Santina?

Queen.

It was a title that loomed somewhere close and yet out of reach. Did she fully understand the responsibility of such a title? Did she have to? Asher didn't know how to be king either—it wasn't something he'd had a practice round for—but Abi knew in the depths of his soul that he would be a good one. Before he had been one in truth, he had already thought like one.

But were they strong enough to figure it out together? Was she the right person for Asher?

It wasn't a matter of whether she was good enough or not. She saw them as equals, and she believed he did too. But would she cause him more trouble than their relationship was worth?

Would Lamberi retaliate and come for her again? Would Lamberi punish Santina because of her?

Abi suppressed a shiver, but it was too strong. Asher shifted, tightening his arms around her, but his eyes remained closed.

Queen.

An enormous responsibility.

An enormous honor.

An enormous title to carry.

Abi had none of the answers, but she knew one thing: she'd always dealt with anything life had thrown her. She'd steered IFRT through more storms than she could've imagined, and she'd kept her wits during her captivity. She hadn't buckled. Her captivity had shown her there was more fight in her than she'd ever imagined.

But it wasn't what a title would do to her that worried her.

Would she be a blessing to Asher?

Or a curse?

Abi pushed the concerns from her mind. No answers would come to her tonight and without a rested mind, she'd only keep going in circles.

She focused her attention on Asher's rhythmic breathing and the steady drum of his heart beneath her ear.

ABI OPENED HER EYES, startled, and it took her a moment to realize what had woken her. Her eyes darted toward the closed door.

Hushed voices.

Her eyes dropped to the crease in the sheets, the only indication Asher had been in bed with her last night.

She threw back the covers and tip-toed toward the door.

"Who did this?" Asher asked in a hushed voice.

"Masked men. The security team is working on it," Jesse said.

"He was a good man," Asher said, sounding pained. "Who else is a target? Everyone I've ever spoken a word to?"

"William Bennett has increased his family's security. He doesn't want our help with that, and he has confidence in his team," Jesse said.

"This has to stop, Jesse," Asher whispered, his eyes going wide. "This has to stop! I won't have any more blood on my hands!" he continued, his voice becoming increasingly wild.

Abi brought her hand to her lips, hating the anguish in Asher's voice.

"It's not on your hands," Jesse said calmly.

"It is! These people are being targeted and dying because of me!" Asher urged.

When Jesse didn't respond, Abi thought they'd left, but she didn't hear any footsteps.

"I'll be back," Jesse said quietly, and Abi heard a door close.

She opened the bedroom door and saw Asher sitting on the couch with his face buried in his hands.

"What's going on?" Abi asked.

Asher looked to her with tormented eyes. "Colonel Stevens was taken from his home last night."

Abi gasped in a breath and her eyes bulged. "What?"

Asher nodded. "His wife woke up to a gunshot and called the police, but he was gone when they arrived, and the footage from their security system has been deleted. Jesse has a crew there now, but there aren't any leads."

Abi noticed her hands were shaking so she held them together in front of her. She hobbled toward Asher, her ankle once again throbbing.

She pried his hands away from his face and threaded her fingers through his.

"He was one of the few people I trusted," Asher said quietly, his eyes staring at the white wall ahead. "And that's why he was targeted."

Abi leaned her head on Asher's shoulder.

She couldn't tell him it was okay or that everything would be all right.

It wasn't—Santina was spiraling out of control.

ASHER

Asher looked at the manicured garden and the white-paned door. It was an idyllic home, but now it was tainted.

Security teams flanked Asher as he walked the path to the front door. It opened as his hand reached for the doorbell, and two red-rimmed eyes met his.

"Mrs. Stevens," Asher said, his throat raw. "I'm so sorry. Your husband is a good man, and we will find him." He didn't know if he believed that, exactly, but he wanted to.

"Thank you, Your Majesty," she said with a voice that sounded like a rasp. She opened the door wide for them.

Asher stepped inside and looked over Colonel Stevens's home office. He wanted to see him there, sitting peacefully at his desk.

"I was home," she said, her voice cracking. "I called the police, but it was too late. He always told me that if something happened to call the police, not to go downstairs . . . I should've done more."

Asher touched her arm. Her skin was cold despite it being a warm summer day. "He would've been thinking of you and been glad you were asleep and safe upstairs," Asher said.

"May I?" Jesse asked from behind him, gesturing toward the office.

"Of course," Mrs. Stevens said, her face blank—and then her eyes bulged. "I'm sorry, Your Majesty, I didn't offer you anything. Would you like a cup of tea?"

Asher gave her a warm smile. "Call me Asher. And please don't apologize—the last thing you need to be worrying about is serving me tea."

Asher's gaze darted to Jesse, who was walking through the office, his head tilting as he looked at certain overturned objects. Asher didn't need to be an investigator to know that the attackers had been looking for something. Colonel Stevens was a military man—a man of order. He would not have kept his office in such disarray.

"Do you have family in Santina, Mrs. Stevens?" Asher asked. He didn't like the idea of her being alone in this house.

"Our daughter lives here," she said with a nod. "She came over this morning, but she's gone home to pick up some clothing. She's going to stay here with me for a few nights."

Asher looked to Jesse, knowing he would be listening.

"Mrs. Stevens," Jesse said, emerging from the office, "we're going to suggest you and your daughter stay in a hotel for a few days—just until we can work out why your husband was taken. There's a chance the men might come back if they didn't find what they were looking for. While that's unlikely, I don't want to rule it out just yet."

Mrs. Steven's eyes narrowed. "What do you think they were looking for?"

"Honestly, I don't know," Jesse said. "But this room has been searched. Did your husband seem concerned about anything last night? Was his behavior different at all?"

Her eyes welled, and then she shook her head. "No. We had dinner and then he came to his office. I went to bed around ten o'clock. He was writing something—a letter, I assume, because he was handwriting it, and he was old-fashioned in that way. He always handwrote his letters." She sucked in a breath and turned away.

Asher looked to Jesse who had turned back to look at the desk.

"I'm sorry," Mrs. Stevens said as she turned away from Asher.

He shook his head. "Please, do not apologize. Your husband was taken last night. If you weren't upset and rattled, I would be concerned."

She inhaled a shuddered breath. "How is the Queen doing?" she asked, then quickly added, "Sorry, I'm probably not supposed to ask."

"Thank you for asking," Asher said, keeping himself calm. "She's stable, and she's fighting. The doctors tell me that's more than I could ask for at this stage, but I just want her to wake up."

Mrs. Stevens gave a sad smile and then blinked, like she was far away. "My husband did say something strange last night. I didn't think much of it until just now. He said, 'Santina is bleeding from the artery.' I assumed he meant because of the war—you know, that we're surrounded by war, and there are talks of you going to war with whoever killed your father. I'm sure you know this . . ." she rambled, her voice trailing off.

Asher didn't know what to make of Mrs. Stevens. She seemed nervous and uncomfortable, but he was hyperaware that she was traumatized and would not be herself today—and wouldn't be for possibly many months, or years, if her husband didn't return. Having the King standing in her home surely wasn't helping matters.

"What did he say?" Jesse asked as he approached them.

"Santina is bleeding from the artery," she repeated hoarsely.

"Okay," Jesse said calmly, but Asher saw something in his eyes. A flicker of something, but then it was gone. "Mrs. Stevens, I'd like to arrange for a team to come over and search your husband's office. I want to make sure we don't miss any clues that will help us find the men who did this, and find your husband."

"Sure, whatever you need," she said.

Jesse looked to his watch. "Can you pack a bag now? I'd like to take you to a hotel. I don't want you to stay here alone."

A tear ran down her cheek. "I suppose. Yes, I can," she said, turning away from them and heading up the stairs.

Jesse pulled out his phone and walked back into the office. He spoke quietly but Asher heard him organize the hotel reservation.

"What does bleeding from the artery mean?" Asher asked quietly.

Jesse's eyes darted to the hallway then back to Asher. "It's a phrase our military uses when the source of danger is coming from a source close to home. In the case of Santina, it would mean the danger to Santina is coming from a Santinian."

Asher narrowed his eyes.

Alistair.

"Don't we know this already?" Asher asked slowly.

Jesse looked into his eyes. "Yes, but the colonel shouldn't have."

Asher paused. Of course the colonel shouldn't have—surprise had flickered in Jesse's eyes, and not because of the phrase, but because someone else knew. What else had the colonel known?

"Right," Asher said, looking over the office again. "Do you think they found what they were looking for?"

"No. I don't think they did . . . If they had, she would be dead," Jesse said.

Asher's eyes widened. "What?" he asked, a hushed whisper.

"They were interrupted by something," Jesse said. "Half this room has been searched carefully—items crooked and out of place. The other half is a mess—items strewn all over the floor and cabinets. My guess is that they would've interrogated Mrs. Stevens next, but for some reason they didn't have a chance. If luck is on our side, we might find what they were looking for."

Asher felt like his luck had run out long ago.

ABI

Abi stared into his bottomless black eyes. Even through the television screen they appeared bottomless—like a deep well. It was unnerving, and she was sure he used that to his advantage when he wanted to.

Rachel and Lenna were sitting on either side of her, and Daniel was sitting beside Rachel. Her eyes landed on the crystal clock on the desk—the King's desk.

"We're going to show you a series of photographs. Please let us know if you recognize any of them," the cute-looking man with glasses said. He'd been introduced as Samuel, but Abi didn't think he looked like one.

"Henry Walter," Abi, Rachel and Daniel said in unison.

Samuel nodded.

The next image flashed on the screen and Abi's teeth ground against one another. "That's my doorman, occasionally," Rachel said.

"He was a guard at my cell in Adani," Abi said.

Samuel nodded again.

A third image flashed. It was the guard who had sat inside the cell with Abi.

The same pattern continued as the faces of another ten or so men flashed onto the screen.

Abi felt eyes watching her, and noticed both James and Samuel were eyeing her carefully.

"Does this man look familiar?" James asked.

Abi took another look.

"No. Who is he?" Abi asked, searching through her mind for a name, but there was nothing familiar about him.

"Lamberi," James said.

Abi's jaw fell open. IFRT had never been able to find an image of him. How had they found it so quickly?

"Are you sure?" Abi asked. "He's impossible to find."

"We're sure," Samuel said. "We don't know where he is, but this is him."

"Huh," Rachel said under her breath beside Abi. "He looks so . . . normal," she eventually said.

Abi had to admit he didn't look like the monster she'd envisioned, either. But that was the thing about dangerous people—sometimes they looked as gentle as kittens.

"How did you find him?" Abi asked. "We've been trying to source an image of him for years."

Samuel cleared his throat. "We have access to some databases that you don't. While we have an image of him, his location is a different matter. We were able to track his whereabouts until two days ago. He hasn't resurfaced since."

"Where was he?" Abi asked.

"Visiting Henry Walter," James said. "Henry was found dead a few hours later." He smirked. "Sometimes criminals do us favors."

James continued. "But what concerns us is this: our early intelligence suggests Henry Walter was the man behind your kidnapping. So, Lamberi killing someone who works for the Adani officials tells us that he is not afraid—and that he is furious that you escaped. We're very concerned about just how furious he is."

"This isn't a surprise," Abi said. "These men are not used to having things taken from them. They do the taking, not the other way around."

James nodded. "Exactly. And he *is* going to try to take back what he considers to be his."

Silence fell over the room. James's words didn't surprise her—she'd known it was a high possibility that Lamberi would retaliate—but the conviction in his voice was undeniable. He spoke as if it were as inevitable as the sun rising tomorrow.

"What do you want me to do?" Abi asked. "I won't sit around and wait for him to attempt to take me or retaliate against Santina as punishment."

James sighed softly, crossing his arms. "At this stage, the best thing we can do is keep you safe and hidden in the palace. If he enters Santina, we need to make a plan. Until then, the best thing we can do is strengthen security and continue to collect intelligence."

"Do you think he will retaliate against Santina?" Abi asked, watching them carefully, but their faces revealed nothing.

"Anything is possible," James said, "but ultimately his focus will be on you."

"And Asher," Abi said, speaking the words James hadn't said. "They all referenced me as 'Asher's girlfriend.' I don't want Asher to pay the price for this mess."

James chewed on his cheek and seemed to be choosing his words. "Abi, what happens next is not your fault. Your captivity aside, the Kingdom of Santina has grave issues. While I don't like the fact that you were taken hostage on the same day as Asher's coronation service—I don't like coincidences—we can't, at this stage, determine that they are connected other than you being mentioned as Asher's girlfriend. Your business is risky, and it's possible that IFRT did something to infuriate Lamberi and he organized this as retaliation against IFRT. Sure, Adani officials are involved, but we don't know why. Did orders come from their king, or has Lamberi infiltrated the government officials? Until we have the answers to these questions, we sit on our hands. I know you won't like this, but if you want to make things as easy for Asher as possible, do what we tell you: stay in the palace.

Don't communicate except via the cell phone Jesse gave you. Don't access your email." He gave an odd smile. "Actually, we've blocked you from your email, so you can't be tempted to make that mistake."

Abi's jaw fell open. She wasn't exactly sure what was on her face, but James seemed to expect it.

"If you make one wrong move, it's very possible you'll end up in Lamberi's arms and Asher will pay for protecting you. Everything we're doing is in your best interest, and Asher's. We're not going to ask for your approval, as that's not how we work. I don't think you'll like—actually, I know you *won't* like—how little control you have. But this is the way we work, and it's why we're successful."

Abi nodded reluctantly, but her mind was still reeling with ways she could help. She couldn't act on anything, but maybe she could suggest ideas and work with them.

"Lenna," Samuel said softly. "Do you know this man?"

Lenna inhaled as her jaw dropped open. Her eyes doubled in size and she began to shake.

Abi looked to the screen, holding her palm out as if to give them a minute.

"Lenna, look at me," Abi said.

The girl shook her head.

"Lenna, it's okay. That man can't hurt you, but I need you to tell me who he is."

"He no hurt me," she said quietly. "He ... my ... father."

Abi's head snapped back to the screen. *How in the world . . .* "Why are you showing her that?" Abi asked not hiding her anger. She was shocked they'd been able to find out who Lenna was and obtain a picture of her father so quickly, and she hardly understood why they would show that to a young girl who had been ripped from everything she'd ever known.

"We needed to see Lenna's reaction," James said without a hint of apology.

"For what?" Abi demanded.

"Because we need to make sure King Asher stays alive," James said, matter-of-factly. "That means that everyone, you included, is being researched and monitored. I won't apologize for this, Abi. Much is at stake, and this is our job."

Abi raised her eyebrows. "I'm not asking you to apologize, but perhaps think about the delivery next time. Lenna was brutally taken from her world and now you flash an image of someone she has only seen in her dreams in front of her and—"

James nodded and held out his palm as if stopping traffic. "It was a test and there was no other way, because it's very hard to test people if they're prepared. It was necessary," he said, gently but firmly.

Abi's jaw jutted out. "What did you learn from your test?"

"That it's been a long time since Lenna has seen her family," James said evenly, but there was much more in his eyes.

Samuel said something under his breath, but Abi didn't catch what it was, and then James nodded. "We're finished for today. Thank you for your time," he said, looking at Abi with careful eyes.

The screen went blank.

Abi sighed and returned her attention to Lenna. "Are you okay?"

"Is he alive?" she asked in a voice that indicated she only wanted to hear one answer.

"I don't know," Abi said. "If he is, we'll find him."

She hesitated before nodding. Abi understood: home was not the place Lenna remembered. War changed everything, and if Lenna went home, she would be forced to face the wreckage of her family. Sometimes it was easier to live in denial.

"I'll speak to them and we'll get more information," Abi said. "Then we'll make a plan." Abi didn't want to make any promises yet because she knew she had to be very careful right now, but if Lenna wanted to go home, Abi would make that possible at the earliest opportunity.

Rachel put a hand on Lenna's shoulder. "But for now, you're late for class," she said with a wink.

Lenna smiled and her big eyes shone. "Sorry, Miss Rachel." She stood and moved toward the door.

Rachel stepped forward, carefully pulling Abi in for a hug. "We have a lunch date, don't forget."

"Of course. I'll check in with Asher and then maybe join you and Lenna before lunch," Abi said.

"How's he holding up?" Rachel asked quietly.

"Actually, better than I expected," Abi admitted. The man she'd seen last night sounded nothing like the man she'd spoken with after Noah's death. Abi knew he'd had some time to process Noah's and his father's deaths, but only a few days. The pain was still raw—and would be for a long time—but Asher was coping.

The corner of Rachel's lips turned up. "That's our king," she said. Her eyes darted behind Abi and Rachel's cheeks tinged pink.

"What about the King?" a voice asked behind Abi.

Abi smiled, turning to face Asher.

"Nothing, Your Majesty," Rachel said with a slight giggle before she excused herself.

"Were you talking about me?" Asher asked with a smile as he strode toward her.

Abi put on her poker face. "I have no idea what you're talking about, Your Majesty."

Asher chuckled as he cupped her face and placed a quick kiss on her lips. "How did the meeting go?"

Abi didn't know where to begin. "Good. I think." Her eyes darted toward the screen, wondering if they were somehow still watching her. "They know things, Asher. The men who held me captive, a photo of Lamberi, Lenna's father . . . It's crazy how much intelligence they've been able to gather already. And it's all accurate."

Asher nodded slowly. "That's why they've been hired. Jesse assured me they're the best in the world."

"Based on that meeting, I'm not doubting that statement," Abi said.

Asher's stomach rumbled. "I need to eat. I couldn't stomach anything this morning."

Abi nodded. "Can we eat outside? I need some fresh air. I've never been in one building for so long; although, this is like a complex of interconnected buildings, so I suppose it doesn't really count."

Abi positioned her crutches and took a step forward. Asher walked patiently beside her.

"How is your ankle this morning?" he asked.

"Better, actually. Hopefully I'll be off these things tomorrow. The doctor came to dress my back and was pleased—the wounds are showing no signs of infection," Abi said.

She let Asher take the lead. She had no idea where they were going, but in that moment she realized this was their future. She would let him lead, and she would trust him even when their destination was uncertain. That didn't mean she would be a wallflower, though. Regardless of any title she carried, she would always be Abigail Bennett at her core.

"This is my mother's favorite garden," Asher said as he led them to an outdoor setting. It was a reflection of everything that was Santina: a slice of modern in a traditional world.

"How many gardens does she have?" Abi asked.

Asher chuckled. "I mean, this piece of garden. They're all one garden, I suppose. In spring, before the heat of summer became too strong, my parents ate breakfast here every morning."

Abi stole a sideways glance. Asher's eyes were raw with pain, and then he shook his head slightly, as if shaking the memories from his mind.

A palace servant arrived carrying a tray of coffee and sweets.

Abi leaned her crutches against the white outdoor sectional and sat down. Asher sat beside her, stretching his legs.

"How did this morning go?" Abi asked gently.

Asher shook his head. "As well as it could've. I think Colonel Stevens knew something about the people who murdered my father."

"Has his house been searched?" Abi asked.

"The new security team is there now, but I'm worried he took it to the grave," Asher said, pouring two cups of coffee.

"Well, if there's something there, I'm sure they'll find it," Abi said, thinking of the meeting she'd just had.

Asher lifted her chin and brought his lips to hers. He moaned as she ran her tongue over his.

He smirked. "God help you when your back is healed."

Abi laughed. "Is that a threat?"

He looked at her with heated eyes. "Don't encourage me, Abi. My self-control is still replenishing after last night."

He ran his fingers through her hair and little bumps spread over her skin. In that moment, they were just Asher and Abi, and she loved it.

A spread of food arrived and Abi salivated at the plates of eggs, fruit and muffins. "Is this how you eat every day?"

Asher gave her an odd look. "Like a hotel buffet? No. I just thought that after everything that's happened it would be nice to have a quiet breakfast together. Don't get used to this," he said with a chuckle. "When I said my parents had breakfast here every morning, that usually consisted of coffee, toast, and a newspaper."

"Your father read the paper every day?" Abi asked. She wondered why. Media reports were often critical of the royal family, and they were also biased and could be untrue. Why would the King subject himself to that every morning?

Asher nodded. "He said that regardless of whether the news reports were accurate, he needed to know what was being said so that he could understand Santina's views."

Abi chewed on her lip. "I don't know, it sounds a bit like torture to me," she said as Jesse emerged from the garden.

"Ash, your mother is awake. She's asking for you," Jesse said.

ASHER

Asher strode through the hospital hallway, almost running. Security guarded the entire wing, and as Asher looked over their faces, he recognized none of them. They stepped aside as he approached the door.

"Your Majesty," one said with a nod.

Asher nodded in return, but he didn't care for pleasantries right now. He wanted to see his mother.

Her eyes landed on him as soon as he stepped inside.

Asher rushed toward her and kissed her forehead. "I'm so glad you're awake," he said.

She balled his T-shirt in her fist as her body began to shake. "They said . . . they said he didn't . . . make . . . it."

Asher drew her in, providing the only comfort he could. She'd fought to wake up, and she'd woken up in hell. He wrapped his arms around her. "He didn't, but we have each other. We'll get through this together," he said, remembering the words they'd spoken before Noah's funeral. Now, his words felt empty.

Her sobs shook her body, and tears slid down his cheeks.

Asher didn't know how long they sat like that, but they both needed it.

Her voice was a wheeze when she spoke. "Are you okay?" she asked, lifting her head to look over him.

"No," Asher said. "But I'm alive, and Santina hasn't fallen in the past few days."

Her eyes narrowed and her gaze drifted off to the right, like she was trying to recall something. "I think you need to call Colonel Stevens."

Asher paused. "What?"

"I don't know . . . I woke up thinking of him, and I feel like he's important, but I don't know why," she said, sounding tired.

Asher turned his mother's face back to him. "Did Father say something in the car that day?"

She paused, seeming to think it through. "I don't know. But I think you should call him."

Asher didn't know if now was the time to tell her, but when would be a good time to tell her?

"Mom, we think he was murdered last night," Asher said gently.

Her eyes doubled in size, and she reached for her throat. "I'm supposed to remember something, Asher, but I can't. It's right there, but I can't grab it."

He squeezed her hands. "It's okay, it'll come to you. You just woke up. You need to rest," he said, but really he needed her to remember.

She suddenly looked back to him. "Where is Alistair?"

"Home," Asher said. *Detained*—but he didn't tell her that.

"Don't let him in here," she said with glistening eyes. "I don't want him here."

"Why?" Asher asked. What did his mother know about Alistair that he didn't?

She looked straight at him. "He killed him."

Asher sat back. He knew Alistair hadn't pulled the trigger because he'd been with Asher when the attack had taken place.

"What do you mean?"

"They said . . ." Her eyes filled with pain and she closed them. "It's the last thing I remember . . ." She opened her eyes slowly, anger filling them before she took a deep breath. "One of them said, 'Alistair said to tell you he's sorry.'"

Asher pulled his mother into his chest as he fought to breathe. He'd known Alistair wasn't clean, but he'd always hoped it was a drug deal gone bad or something else that had forced his involvement. *What kind of person organizes the murder of their own parents?*

"I'll take care of this," Asher said, his voice low and guttural. "I'm going to make this right."

His mother sobbed in his arms. "It was the first time I'd ever seen your father truly scared . . ." Her voice trailed off, muffled by Asher's chest.

Asher shook his head furiously as tears ran down his cheeks. "You did nothing to deserve this. You were better parents than we could've asked for. Something is very wrong with Alistair."

An image of Alistair as a child flashed in his mind. Where had things gone so wrong?

She inhaled a shaky breath and straightened, wiping away her tears. "I'm sorry, I shouldn't have . . ."

Her mask was back on, but Asher didn't want to see a composed queen—he wanted to see his mother.

"Mom," he said, taking her hand. "Don't do that. Don't push me out. We'll get through this together. We stick together," Asher said. *Because we're all that's left.*

She gave a small nod.

"Emma Bennett has been here," Asher said, hoping the news would give his mother some comfort. "She's been taking turns sitting with you. She'll be very happy to see you awake."

Emilia's voice was a whisper. "I thought I'd dreamt that."

"No, she's been right by your side," Asher said, and his mother began to sob again. This time they were tears of joy, or at least relief, he assumed.

"It's the saddest thing about our world . . . It takes a tragedy for us humans to remember what's important," she said, sounding far away as she looked to the small window. "And we usually remember too late. One of your father's best qualities was his ability to live in the present. He didn't look back, and he didn't worry about the future. He focused on the present and the people he loved."

A knock at the door interrupted them. Asher turned and called out, "Come in."

A door opened to reveal Emma Bennett standing beside Jesse. She took one look at them and shook her head. "I'm sorry—I'll come back."

Asher shook his head. "No, please come in. I need to attend to a few things," he said, standing. He kissed his mother's forehead. "I'll be back soon."

A security guard stepped inside with Emma Bennett and Asher stole a look over his shoulder as the door closed behind him. He saw his mother and her best friend embrace with tears streaming down their cheeks.

"I want to see Alistair," Asher said.

ALISTAIR

Alistair turned on the faucet and let the water run. His gaze lifted to the ceiling, looking for cameras. He couldn't lose his security team no matter how hard he tried—and he had. They were like shadows, and they weren't the only shadows Alistair had.

He kneeled on the tiled floor and slowly opened the vanity doors. If they'd found this phone, he didn't know what he was going to do. He examined the contents of the cabinet, but everything looked to be in order. He'd strategically placed several items on angles, and he knew looking at them now that they hadn't been moved. He pushed them aside quickly and unscrewed the plastic ring that connected two pieces of piping for the second basin. Alistair grunted under his breath. Why was it so tight? He needed a tool, but he could hardly get his hands on one without security noticing. He wiped the sweat off his brow. He was on the edge and he needed another hit. He needed it soon, or all pretenses that he'd stopped using would be over.

He pulled his sleeve over his hand and tried again. It moved a fraction. Alistair gave it one last turn and, finally, it opened. He spun the ring loose and it dropped down, opening up the pipes. He contorted his fingers, reaching until he felt the thin plastic bag. He yanked it loose with another grunt. His eyes darted to the door—it was locked and it couldn't be opened from the outside, but he didn't think security would hesitate to kick it in if they thought he was up to something.

He moved fast, opening the ziplock bag full of powder and a burner phone. He grabbed the small spoon from the bag and took a hit. The hot burn through his nostrils and the acrid residue in his throat made him feel better instantly. He took a small dose, enough but not too much that someone would notice he was high. He'd been a functioning addict for years—much longer than anyone realized.

He could think again.

He grabbed the phone and checked his messages. There were seventeen of them, and they were all from the same sender.

A bang on the door made him jump and he almost threw the phone.

"Alistair, come on!"

Alistair's heart was in his throat. With shaky hands, he opened the last message.

Keep your mouth shut, or he dies.

Alistair's mouth went dry. It wasn't a false threat. Last time he'd ignored it, his parents had been targeted.

He typed a quick response:

My lips are sealed. Fuck off.

He turned off the phone and put it back in the bag with his remaining supply. He only had a month at best, so that gave him a few weeks to figure out how to get another bag without Jesse finding out.

He grabbed the soap box which concealed a roll of tape. His eyes darted between the door and the bag in his hands. He taped the bag to the pipe, put the soap box back on a strategic angle he'd remember, and then closed it as a loud bang came from the door.

Alistair opened it to see Jesse standing there, his fist ready to break down the door. He didn't say a word, but his eyes said everything. Jesse knew Alistair was up to something.

"Everything all right?" Jesse asked, his gaze boring into Alistair.

It took everything not to flinch. He'd never been more thankful for the hit he'd taken a few seconds ago—it was keeping him calm.

"Fine," Alistair responded. "I felt sick. I needed to splash some water on my face."

Jesse nodded and stepped aside, motioning for Alistair to leave the bathroom.

Alistair couldn't take a piss without permission.

He rolled his eyes at Jesse but moved along. He'd done what he'd needed to and bought himself another few days.

He went outside, needing some fresh air. The Santinian sun beamed down, warming his cold soul. He felt cold all the time now. At first he'd thought it was just a withdrawal symptom, and it likely was in part; he wasn't clean, but he'd significantly reduced how much he'd been using, though not by choice. He knew it was also more than that, though—his soul was cold to the core. He was dead inside, and he was nothing more than a functioning corpse.

He heard someone talking and knew it was Asher. Alistair turned and walked in the opposite direction. He had no desire to see his brother, or Abigail Bennett.

He looked over his shoulder to see a full security team behind him. There were a few new faces, but Alistair didn't give that much more thought. Jesse was pulling out all the stops to keep King Asher alive so Alistair had expected security to tighten. He was glad it had. If they were watching Alistair, it would also keep him safe. He'd been looking over his shoulder for the past twelve months and that fear had taken its toll. Everyone wondered why he'd spiraled out of control, but the answer was simple: fear.

He still remembered the night he'd racked up enough lines to overdose. He'd thought that a better alternative than living in constant fear. If he'd known how the following six months would turn out, he would've done it. Of course, the drugs only made him more paranoid, but Alistair had every reason to be paranoid in the first place.

"Alistair! Alistair!"

Alistair stopped, slowly turning to face his brother. The King. His face remained impassive, but his blood boiled. Asher was a mirror of everything Alistair should've been.

"Your Majesty," Alistair said, his words drowning in contempt.

To Asher's credit, he ignored it.

"Mother is awake," Asher said.

"When?" Alistair asked quickly.

"This morning. I just got home from the hospital," Asher said.

So his brother had been and gone, and only now he thought to tell Alistair their mother was awake. Alistair didn't know why he was surprised.

"How is she?" he asked, uneasy. He felt itchy and nauseous.

Asher's eyes hardened. "She has some memory loss, but otherwise she's doing as well as can be expected."

"Good," Alistair said. "That's good."

Asher scrutinized him, like he was searching for the secrets he knew Alistair was hiding. But Asher had no idea. None at all.

A long pause followed.

Eventually, Asher said, "She asked not to see you. She said you killed her husband, *our* father."

Alistair's eyes widened and a wave of nausea rolled through him. "What?" he asked, his voice a gasp. His hand went to his mouth as if he was ready to catch his own vomit, or try to hold it in. That thought incited another wave of nausea.

Asher's voice was chilling when he spoke next.

"Take him," Asher instructed, and the security team moved in.

ASHER

"I'm the only brother you have left," Alistair hissed.

Those seven words lit a fire of fury in Asher's chest. He lunged, grabbed an unprepared Alistair by the collar, and smashed his fist into his brother's nose.

Pain shot through Asher's hand and blood sprayed across Alistair's T-shirt. It took a moment for his brother to recover from the shock—Asher wasn't normally one to throw punches. He raised his fist for another strike, but Jesse stepped in as two hands grabbed Asher by the waist, pulling him back.

"Enough!" Jesse warned, with one hand pressed against Alistair's chest. "Enough," he repeated.

Alistair's eyes blazed and Asher wondered if his brother was as furious as he was, or if it was Asher's own reflection in his brother's eyes.

"What the fuck?!" Alistair swore as he brushed a hand across his cheek, smearing the blood.

"And whose fault is it that Noah is dead?" Asher asked, his voice scathing. "Lock him up!" Asher demanded as he stormed away, noting his own T-shirt had been sprayed with blood.

Jesse was right beside him like a shadow he couldn't lose as Asher went to his living quarters and found another shirt.

"You need to cool off," Jesse said calmly.

"He deserved it," Asher said, aware he sounded like a petulant child.

"Agreed, which is why I didn't stop you. But now that's out of your system, we need to talk about what happens next," Jesse said.

"Put him in prison where he belongs. Death is too good for him," Asher said, his anger like a hot iron rod searing his throat.

"Or, perhaps we should convince him to talk so we can actually find out what happened. Alistair didn't do this alone," Jesse said, obviously thinking much more clearly than Asher.

Asher sighed as he balled up his ruined shirt and threw it in the laundry hamper. "What do you suggest?"

"Interrogation. He needs to be motivated to talk, because he's not going to incriminate himself willingly," Jesse said.

"Do it. I want it done today. Now," Asher said. He couldn't live like this—in constant fear, always looking over his shoulder.

Jesse nodded. "I'll do it myself."

Asher pressed his palms against the wall. He needed to think straight, needed to think like a king, but all he could see was red.

He squeezed his eyes shut and tilted his head back to the ceiling. He'd broken Alistair's nose for sure—he'd heard the bone crunching as his fist connected with it.

He looked over his stained knuckles and went to the bathroom to wash the blood off his hands. The basin turned red.

Asher sighed as he looked in the mirror. Shadows lined his eyes and he was surprised his hair hadn't turned gray.

Asher changed into a fresh shirt and nodded to Jesse's replacement. "I want to watch," Asher said.

* * *

ASHER STARED at the television screen on the wall in his office. Alistair was seated in a chair with his limbs bound, dried blood trailing from his nose to his lip.

Even from where Asher sat, the look Alistair gave Jesse was chilling.

"You've been implicated in the murder of Noah and your father, the attempted murder of your mother, and aiding in the abduction of Abigail Bennett. If you want to live to see tomorrow, make this easy for yourself."

Alistair scoffed.

"The problem is, you see me as Jesse," Jesse said, his voice low. "And that's a mistake. Right now, I'm not the man you know. I'm a man who's angry and grieving—a man who's prepared to do whatever needs to be done to bring the King's killer to justice."

"You're wasting your time," Alistair said with hard eyes.

Jesse paused, and then slammed a knife into Alistair's hand. He bucked, throwing his head back and howling.

Asher grimaced but didn't look away.

"I don't think I am," Jesse said, turning the knife.

Alistair ground his teeth together, sucking in a violent breath. "Fuck you!"

Asher couldn't see Jesse's face but he saw the tightening of his shoulders.

A moment passed, and then Jesse moved so fast Asher almost missed it—but the damage he did was unmistakable.

A red line parted the flesh of Alistair's cheek and blood fell from the wound like a red waterfall. It dripped onto the floor.

"Whatever you think you know," Alistair said, breathless, "you don't. I didn't kill my father, and I didn't kill Noah."

"I don't believe you," Jesse said without hesitation. "Make me. Tell me what you know, because there's a lot more to you than the reckless, party-animal version of Alistair you've been putting on display."

Alistair raised an eyebrow. "Really? My father thought otherwise."

"You gave your father no choice," Jesse said matter-of-factly. His voice was unusually cold. Emotionless. It gave Asher the chills, and he hoped it was beginning to break down Alistair's walls.

"He saw what he wanted to see. Everyone did—*King* Asher included," Alistair said bitterly.

"What did you want them to see?" Jesse asked, his voice a little warmer.

"That I needed help. But what did I get instead? Criticism," Alistair said, his eyes blazing.

"Help from the drugs?" Jesse asked.

Asher shifted restlessly. He didn't care about Alistair and his drug problem—they knew all about that.

Asher swallowed his frustration like a bitter pill. Interrogation was not his specialty, and he knew better than to step in. He folded his arms over his chest and watched on impatiently.

"Of course from the drugs," Alistair said, impatiently. "I've been clean for weeks now, and no one has even noticed."

"Actually, everyone noticed," Jesse said. "The problem is your timing. You've had a very unusual response to your father's death. Most people with a drug addiction would spiral further into despair, but you chose this time to pull yourself out of a hole. You've shown no signs of grief, or anything else."

Alistair's eyes narrowed. "What do you want me to do? Weep in the corner for the man who despised me?"

Jesse pulled a knife and slashed Alistair's other cheek. He howled again, spewing a string of profanities.

"What I want is for you to cut the crap and start talking," Jesse told him. "Tell me about the oil you discovered at the ruins and why you didn't tell King Asher about it."

Alistair blinked, clearly surprised, and Asher realized the man had thought his secret was still under wraps. "King Martin should've told Asher. That's not my job."

"King Martin didn't have a chance, did he?" Jesse asked through gritted teeth.

Asher's jaw clenched.

Alistair's eyes hardened. "It doesn't matter now. The deal has been done."

"What deal?" Jesse asked.

Asher didn't know if he knew and was asking just to hear it from Alistair, or if Jesse actually had no idea. His voice gave away nothing.

"The deal I brokered for Santina," Alistair said with a smirk. "But there's one contingency to that deal: I must stay alive. They hail King Asher, but I'm the one who will be remembered. I'm the one who will save Santina."

Jesse moved quickly, holding a knife to Alistair's throat. "Stop fucking around and start talking before I slit your damn throat."

"I sold it," Alistair said slowly. "I sold the ruins and the oil wells to Adani. Santina will never be hungry again."

Asher jolted like he'd been stung by a wasp.

"What do you mean you sold it?" Jesse shouted, his voice scathing. All calmness was gone.

"Hail Crown Prince Alistair," Alistair said with a smirk. "I was Crown Prince and I negotiated the deal. Father was too weak—he would never have allowed the sale of the holy land. I did what needed to be done."

Jesse shook his head slowly. "You're a fucking idiot. Where are the sale documents?"

"The deal is done," Alistair said.

"Where are the documents?" Jesse asked, turning the knife in Alistair's thigh.

Alistair grunted as he wheezed in a breath. He gave a pained laugh. "Underneath my bed. Seriously."

Jesse stood abruptly and his chair fell over behind him. "I'm going to find those documents, and if they're signed with the King's stamp, God help you," he said through gritted teeth.

"Remember the part of the deal that says I must be alive," Alistair said airily.

"Alive and well are two very different things," Jesse said before striding toward the door.

His eyes landed on Asher as he emerged into the office but his words were directed at his team. "Search Alistair's living quarters."

Everyone scuttled like fleeing mice and Jesse met Asher's gaze.

"If the documents are signed with the King's stamp," Asher said, "and the King is dead, the contract can't be contested, can it?"

Jesse shook his head. "No. If it is stamped, it's Adani land now.

Alistair is right. Your father would never have agreed to this, and with good reason—but he's also right about the money. If he brokered a good deal, Santina will never be hungry again."

"But at what cost?" Asher exclaimed. "Adani would be a step closer to taking Santina," he said, his hand going to his throat. He felt like the walls were closing in. "How did he do this? I've seen Alistair make deals and he's not a strong negotiator. He didn't do this alone. Someone helped him, Jesse, and I need you to find out who that was."

"What do you want me to do with him?" Jesse asked. "He should be kept alive for now."

Asher looked to the screen, his eyes landing on his pathetic excuse for a brother. "Get the name of the person who helped him broker this deal, then put him in a cell. Give him the same courtesies Abi was given."

Jesse nodded then looked at his watch. "You're due to go to the hospital in an hour for your MRI. Doctor's orders," Jesse said quickly, like he expected Asher to object.

"I'll check in with Abi, and then I'll meet you in the dining room. I want to know as soon as those documents are found," Asher said stridently.

"Sure," Jesse said. "Give me ten minutes to deal with Alistair and I'll come find you."

Jesse nodded to the men lining the walls of the office. They escorted Asher to the dining room.

As Asher approached, he held back, lingering in the doorway. Abi hadn't seen him and he took a moment to watch her. She sat beside Lenna, and Rachel sat opposite them.

Lenna was writing and they looked on with smiles.

"What happens next?" Abi asked, her eyes lingering on the paper underneath Lenna's hands.

"He dies," Lenna said. From where he stood, Asher could only see written words on the paper. Had she been writing a story?

Abi frowned. "Why?"

"Because the good ones don't live. Only the bad ones," Lenna said.

Asher wondered if that was the truest thing he'd ever heard.

ASHER

*H*e held the papers in his trembling hands. They were stamped, and the Lithe ruins were no longer Santina's.

Asher's blood boiled.

Not only had Alistair attempted to murder their parents, he'd fraudulently sold holy land, the ruins that were to be Santina's next tourism attractions, and Asher's favorite place in the Kingdom.

Alistair thought he'd be hailed for saving Santina, but what he hadn't fully considered was the backlash from Santinians for selling their land to Adani. Alistair's thinking had been short-sighted—he hadn't considered the long-term income of a tourist destination, and he hadn't considered the impact of Adani's influence over their border controls.

Martin Snider. That was the name Alistair had given—the name of the man who had helped him broker the deal. The problem was, they had no idea who Martin Snider was.

Asher groaned, burying his face in his hands. He hadn't thought things could get any worse. How wrong he'd been.

He put the papers aside and opened the stack of mail on his desk. He read through the condolence letters and dictated response letters.

He paused when he opened the letter from the Adani King and Crown Prince.

His teeth ground as he read the words.

He dictated a very different response to the other condolences letters.

Your Majesty and Your Royal Highness,

Thank you for your condolence letter. In the time since the passing of my father, and the kidnapping of Abigail Bennett, my position on our relationship has changed.

Santina ceases all alliances with Adani.

We are not foolish, and we are not stupid. We do not wish any harm to come to Adani, but we will fight for what is our own—this includes the Lithe ruins, the sale of which was brokered illegally without the consent of King Martin. The King's stamp was unauthorized and we will not be handing over the ruins or any of the land included in the deal. The broker of this deal has been charged with treason.

I will not tolerate liars, murderers, or anyone who intends to harm Santina.

Regards,

King Asher

Asher replayed the message and his heart broke again. Asher had to set an example, had to scare his enemies. He wanted them to feel a slither of his fear—of his pain.

His gaze lifted as Jesse strode in.

"Can I have a minute?" Jesse asked.

"Sure," Asher said, putting his Dictaphone aside.

"Our search of Colonel Steven's office didn't result in any hard evidence, but we did review his diary—he kept a paper diary with his appointments. He met with someone called HW a week before Abi was taken hostage."

Asher's eyes narrowed. "Who is HW?"

Jesse grimaced. "Henry Walker—a key interest in Abi's kidnapping. Stevens recorded the location and time, and the security team has verified the meeting via security footage and confirmed Henry Walker was in Santina. Midnight was an odd time for a meeting, and it was strange that Colonel Stevens would be meeting with him at all. We're trying to establish who initiated the meeting and what was discussed. The table they were seated at was in a blind spot, which was likely not an accident. Henry Walker is known as a 'black mark'—someone who has no official association with the Adani government but does jobs for them that they don't want to be linked to."

"Why would a man like that even be allowed to enter Santina?" Asher asked slowly.

Jesse sighed. "I don't know, and I can't think of a good reason why Colonel Stevens would've been meeting him, but it's likely that the colonel also permitted his entry into Santina. He is no longer a threat, though—Henry Walker is dead. He was murdered a few nights before the colonel. Whatever the reasons for their meeting, both men knew something they shouldn't—something someone is prepared to kill for."

"What is Thomas Security saying about this?" Asher asked, his mind reeling.

"That they need more information. Which brings me to the real reason for this chat: now that your mother is awake, they think it's in your best interest to hold the public ceremony for your father. They want to see which of your 'friends' turn up to pay their respects, and then they want to use that opportunity to follow them, get tags on them, and see who they speak to. Every step they take and every word they speak will be monitored."

Asher raised an eyebrow. "Are they actually capable of doing that?"

Jesse nodded. "They say they can. They're all flying in for it, once you give the go-ahead. They want to be onsite for security purposes, and to handle the logistics of such an operation."

Asher sighed. "Okay. When do they want to do it?"

"They said that's your call, but the sooner the better." Jesse took a deep breath. "And, Asher—they want Abigail Bennett, and her father, by your side. They believe that will send a very strong message to your enemies that you're not afraid."

"You said yourself that Abi doesn't need any media attention right now," Asher said with a raised eyebrow.

"That was correct a few days ago," Jesse admitted. "I didn't want her photographed getting off the plane. Her ankle is coming along well and with another week of rest the doctor thinks she'll be able to walk on it. A good makeup artist will be able to hide what's left of her bruising and cut lip. I think we should set the public funeral for a week from tomorrow. That will give your mother some more time to prepare herself, will give security time to assemble, and will give your enemies time to clear their schedules—because we want them all here."

Asher thought it through for a moment and then nodded. He wanted the public funeral over with—the sooner the better—and if it provided any of the intelligence they so desperately needed, that was a good thing too.

"Okay," Asher said. "A week from tomorrow." His gaze dropped to the Dictaphone and he removed the tape. He would save that letter for after the funeral. He wanted Adani officials to attend—he wanted to look them straight in the eye and look at his father's killers. He wanted to show them they had underestimated him.

Asher was going to show the world what happened when Santina was threatened.

Jesse nodded then excused himself.

Asher picked up his Dictaphone again to prepare a speech he didn't know how he would deliver.

It is with pain and sorrow that I bid farewell to my father, King Martin.

ASHER

A knock at the door interrupted him yet again. He was expecting Jesse, but Abi entered and he felt the tension melt from his body.

"Hey," he said, holding out arms for her.

She paused, seeming to take him in for a moment. She moved toward him with ease, despite having to use the crutches.

"Come here," Asher said, his voice noticeably lower. He really needed to write his father's obituary, he knew, but Abi was a welcome distraction from the weight of that duty.

He leaned her crutches against his desk and guided her onto his lap. His lips brushed against hers, and for a moment everything was okay.

"How does it feel sitting here?" she asked gently, her hand cupping his cheek.

He sighed. "Foreign, uncomfortable. I feel like an intruder in my father's office."

She looked over the desk, a desk still occupied with his father's things. He couldn't bring himself to pack them away.

"Why don't you make a new office? Make one that is yours," she suggested gently.

"Because I'm scared I'll lose him," Asher said with a shake of his head. "I know it doesn't make any sense, but at least in this office—where he spent most of his time—I can almost feel his presence, and I pray he's guiding me. If I move to another office, there will be no reminders of him, no presence, and then I'll be completely on my own. So, I think this is the lesser of the two evils."

She kissed his forehead. "I don't think I've ever told you how amazing I think you are, Asher. I believe in you, and I'll always have your back."

He closed his eyes, relishing in her touch. It heated his body and calmed his soul. He wondered if his mother had the same effect on his father.

"The public funeral will be held in one week," Asher said, pulling back so he could see her eyes. He watched her carefully, looking for any sign of hesitation—any indication she wasn't ready—but saw less than he'd expected. "Security has advised that we should arrive together," he explained. "They want to see how Santina and our enemies react."

"Wow. Okay," she said. "Do you think that's a good idea?"

"I think the sooner I face this, get answers and deal with those involved, the better," Asher said.

Abi nodded. "Okay," she repeated, still sounding unsure. "If you think it's a good idea, I'll be by your side."

He drew her in, needing her closer. He threaded his hands through her hair, angling her lips to his. She made him feel powerful, made him feel like they could conquer the world. And they damn well might have to.

"Obviously, there'll be no hiding our relationship after that," he said. "Are you sure about this? About us?"

He expected another pause, another uncertain answer.

Abi shook her head heavily. "I've never been unsure about you. I'm still worried about my past, and if it will cause problems for you, but if the security team thinks they can handle that"—she smiled, meeting his eyes—"then I'm all in."

Asher kissed her, pouring all his fear and worries into that kiss.

Her tongue swept over his and his body reacted, begging for more. Her hands ran through his hair, tugging it like she, too, couldn't get enough.

His office phone rang like a shrill siren. He cleared his throat.

"King Asher speaking," he said, his hand tightening on Abi's hip. He didn't want her to move an inch.

"Asher, this is James Thomas. I need a minute of your time. Please ask Abi to leave," he said, his voice calm but urgent at the same time. It was unnerving.

He hesitated, then put the phone on his desk.

"Give me a few minutes. I'll come and find you," he said.

"Sure," she said without pause. She kissed him, then ran her thumb over his lips. "See you soon," she said with a smile before gliding out of his office.

Asher returned his attention to the phone call. This had better be good.

"James," Asher said.

"Thank you," James said. "I want to let you know we'll be attending the funeral. All security procedures are in place, but I want to be there myself—I want to see with my own eyes what's going on."

Asher paused. "Right," he said, still wondering if this was strange, or standard protocol for James Thomas.

"But that's not the reason for my call," James said. "I'm going to brief you directly on this situation from now on. Jesse can communicate with me as he needs, but you'll be the only one fully briefed. And if you see or feel anything concerning, the same applies—you come to me, you don't go to Jesse. Understood?"

Asher's spine tingled. "Is there a problem with Jesse?"

"I don't know," James said simply. "We're running into blocks getting data, more than usual. That means that they—it's likely more than one person—are working with your enemies. I'm not saying one of those people is Jesse, but until I can absolutely clear him, any concerns come to me."

But that wasn't enough for Asher, not now. "How much do you trust Jesse right now?" he asked, keeping his words calm.

"Based on the intelligence we have been able to uncover, I have no reason to suspect him of foul play," James answered, his voice warming slightly. "And Jesse was the one who requested to bring us in. Anyone who knows us knows that we're the best—so if Jesse was involved, it would be a really stupid move on his part to do so. Then again, sometimes desperate people do desperate things. I'm not ruling him out yet; in fact, the only two people that are ruled out are you and your mother. As far as I'm concerned, everyone else is still under suspicion."

Asher felt his defenses rise. "Abi included. That's why you told me to ask her to leave."

"This isn't personal, Asher," James said coolly. "If someone you know—especially someone close to you—has something to hide, you're better off knowing it now rather than later." Asher thought he picked up a trace of pain in James's words. *Maybe James Thomas is speaking from experience.*

"Anything else?" Asher asked. His mood was souring by the second, even though he knew the other man was right.

"Yes. Martin Snider is an alias, of that much we're sure. We're continuing to work on this lead—and we have reason to suspect that the colonel is still alive," James said.

Asher's jaw dropped open—both at the revelation, and at the casualness of James Thomas's voice.

"How?" Asher said hoarsely.

"Pieces of communication we've intercepted. I don't have anything definite as yet, but there's talk of a hostage in Santina. We think it's him."

Asher's mind was reeling. "Who knows about this? Have you told his wife?"

"No one knows, including Jesse, and certainly not his wife. I don't want to get her hopes up until I know we can deliver him home alive. This is a test now, and we'll see who passes. We're working on some other leads, but at this stage, Colonel Stevens is our key focus. I told you this only to give you confidence that we know what we're doing and you can trust us to get to the bottom of this. We were recommended to you, but other than that, you had very little to base your decision on. I'm aware of that, and of the level of trust you've placed in us. You need to know we're capable, so I'll brief you as we go along." James paused, and his next words were full of warning. "If you want to stay alive, and you want to protect Abi, do everything I tell you."

"Understood," Asher said, knowing James had thrown Abi in there for effect. Asher knew it was easier to make a reckless decision when it would only impact his own life.

"Asher, I need to go, but I want to also let you know I'm sending one of my guys in to work directly with Jesse. His name is Reed, and you'll meet him soon. If you have questions, call me or speak to him. That's it—don't speak to anyone else about your security concerns. I'll let you know when Jesse has been cleared. We're working on it, I promise, and in the meantime I've placed more of my men on site. You'll be seeing a few unfamiliar faces the next time your team walks through the door. I'll talk to you soon," James said, and the line went silent.

Asher placed the phone back on the receiver, trying to absorb everything he'd been told in the last few minutes.

Was the colonel still alive?

And if he was, was he being tortured?

There was a knock at his door before it opened. His security team entered and Asher scanned the faces of the men.

A few unfamiliar faces?

He barely recognized any of them.

RACHEL

Rachel cradled the cup of tea in her hands and looked over the headquarters of IFRT. It was the first time she'd left the palace since they'd found Abi, and Rachel thought she'd be able to enjoy a minute alone. But that minute wasn't giving her the sense of peace she'd expected. Her eyes scanned their dingy office and she felt like she was sitting in ruins. It wasn't the physical appearance of the office—that hadn't changed—but everything else had.

What would become of IFRT now that Abi couldn't lead it?

Rachel scrolled through the organization's emails. The team had been monitoring them, but anything that couldn't be actioned had been filed in an electronic folder, and the folder was almost full: full of emails from civilians, authorities, dignitaries, and even a few celebrities wanting to partner with them. If any good had come from Abi's kidnapping, it had been the raising of IFRT's profile in the media.

King Asher's girlfriend—the humanitarian—kidnapped.

But now some hard decisions had to be made.

The rest of the world hadn't stopped just because theirs had. People were still being kidnapped, and if the latest reports were anything to go by, the kidnappings had increased.

Was that a coincidence?

Or was that retaliation?

The talk of a war was increasing too. However much Asher's family had fallen out of favor with Santinians, they still weren't happy their king had been assassinated, and ever since Asher's speech on the balcony, whispers of a war had started.

Rachel knew that was an internal struggle for Asher. His father had worked so hard to keep the war from Santina, but if he didn't retaliate, he'd be perceived as weak. He'd told the world those responsible would be punished, and now King Asher had to do exactly that.

Rachel sighed, taking a sip of her tea.

If she'd thought they had problems before, now they really did.

That thought disappeared the instant she heard the faint, familiar sound of a car engine. Her eyes darted to the security footage of the areas surrounding their building.

Her pulse quickened and her mouth went dry. A car had pulled up without its lights on at midnight and that told her only one thing—whoever was in that car didn't want to be seen.

Three figures emerged from the vehicle and Rachel's breath caught in her throat. She wasn't expecting visitors and her security team wasn't due to pick her up for another thirty minutes.

She darted toward the desk and grabbed her gun. She struggled to swallow. She couldn't believe she'd been stupid enough to come here alone—or that her security team had dropped her off and left her. How good was this team, really?

Rachel knew the sound of a lock being picked, and she held her breath, counting the seconds. If these guys were professionals, it should only take them a few seconds.

It took them less than thirty, and the lock on the back door was a good one—it wasn't some cheap thing they'd bought at the hardware store.

Rachel moved to the closest wall and pressed her back against it, her pistol in her hands. But her hands were beginning to tremble.

With a shaky breath, she aimed the pistol away from her feet. The last thing she needed was to accidentally shoot herself.

The door swung open at the same time a figure emerged from the corner of the room.

Her sharp intake of breath burned her lungs.

Fear was an ugly monster, and it was real. Whoever had said fear was just in the mind had never experienced it, not truly.

She aimed her weapon, but her finger never pulled the trigger.

Her breath was stolen from her as people—she couldn't count how many—moved so fast she couldn't keep track of them. One yelled, another hissed and grunted as they fought. A bullet fired and she shrank back, fighting to breathe.

She couldn't look away as her protector from the shadows took down the intruders within seconds with a few swift moves. He moved like someone out of *The Matrix*.

Before she knew it, a hand wrapped around her mouth and she fought against it.

"It's cold outside," a voice whispered calmly.

Rachel felt the fight leave her as the words registered in her mind —it was the code she'd been given in the event she found herself in this situation and didn't know who to trust. If she heard those words —*it's cold outside*—she knew they were the new security team. Strong arms wrapped around her waist and drew her back to the corner. Moments later, gunshots rang and men started yelling and shouting before it all went quiet again.

"Copy," the voice beside her whispered before releasing her.

She turned to face him, but she could barely make out his features before he was striding forward. She watched him walk toward the men who were now on their knees, their hands behind their heads, pistols pointed at them.

Within seconds, Rachel knew the Matrix man was the one in charge. The guy who had silenced her must have been second-in-charge, because he was giving orders now too.

"Tie them up and gag them. We're taking them with us."

American—Rachel knew from his accent. She hadn't noticed it when he'd first spoken to her, when he'd whispered in her ear, but in her defense, panic had consumed her, and she'd barely been able to remember to breathe. Luckily, the human body was intelligent enough to do that without her having to instruct it to; but fear also had a way of knocking the breath right out of the lungs.

The team moved with a sense of ease and coordination that Rachel had never seen before.

Who are these guys?

When the men were bound and gagged and being dragged off, the first-in-command turned to Rachel.

She blinked when she saw him in the light. Now was not the time for such feelings, but they came anyway.

Holy hell.

He strode toward her and extended his hand. "Apologies for the lack of notice—we're good at that," he said, the corners of his pink lips turning up. His baby-face surprised her—it didn't match his lethal performance.

"And you are?" Rachel asked, amazed she managed to push the words from her throat. Her voice had that husky, sexy thing going on, and none of it was intentional.

"Thomas Security," he said, like it was the most obvious thing in the world. She knew that, but she wanted his name.

"Reed," he said with mischievous eyes. "I'm Reed." A slight beard highlighted his angled jaw and her eyes traced it. He didn't miss it.

She shook his hand, hoping her hand wasn't sweaty, which she was almost certain it was.

"Rachel," she said, even though he of course knew who she was. "When did you enter this building? You didn't come in with the security team that dropped me off," she said.

He raised an eyebrow, perhaps at her tone. "I came in a few hours ago. Did you really think security would scope the office and then let you stay here alone?"

She had thought that was irresponsible, but she'd needed a moment alone, so she hadn't questioned it. She'd assumed they were outside, somewhere close.

Reed looked over his shoulder, nodded, and then turned back to her. She noted one ear was pierced with a small stud.

"Let's get back to the palace. I'll brief you on the way," he said. His brown eyes changed with the tone of his voice—more gentle now.

"Let me just grab a few things," she said quickly. She put her laptop in her handbag and grabbed the file on the desk, the file Abi had asked for.

"I'm ready," she said, grabbing her keys.

They left via the front door, but Rachel couldn't help looking over her shoulder one last time. She hadn't seen the faces of the intruders, and now the security team was blocking her view.

Reed placed his hand on her lower back. "Keep moving," he said.

Rachel suppressed a shiver. There was nothing sexual in his intent, but his touch and his deep voice whispering in her ear sent a strange energy through her. Rachel dismissed the thought—her mind was just reeling from the adrenaline.

As they stepped outside, she saw another security team waiting for her. Reed nodded and they moved in, escorting Rachel to the car.

Jesse's security had been one thing. This was another level completely.

Reed slid in next to her. "Go," he said to the driver.

"Who were they?" Rachel asked.

Reed shrugged. "I'm not sure yet. The team will talk to them and find out."

Rachel smirked at his choice of word. "*Talk*, huh?"

She watched Reed closely and thought he was hiding a smile. "Don't pretend you're all innocent. I've read your report and you're certainly no wallflower."

Her jaw fell open, but the reprimand on her lips vanished when she saw the look in his eyes. Appreciation?

Reed didn't like wallflowers, perhaps?

"Is that so? And what report is this?" Rachel asked.

"Security intelligence report. Everyone has one," he said simply.

"In your world everyone has one," she corrected.

"And yet our worlds collide," he said, but his eyes were on the mirror.

"Problem?" she asked, her gaze following his.

"No, just checking," he said.

Rachel shook her head, as if to clear her jumbled thoughts. She needed to get her mind back on track. "Did the men look familiar to you?"

"No," he said, checking the mirrors again. "But we received a tipoff through some communication that IFRT's headquarters might be targeted tonight. We didn't have all the information we required, so we planted men—myself and a few others—in the building some hours ago. Your security team dropped you off and left so anyone watching would think you were alone."

"I haven't seen you around the palace," Rachel said. She definitely hadn't seen him before tonight—she would've remembered him.

"No, I flew in a few hours ago. James wanted an extra set of hands on site," he said.

"And James put you in charge?" Rachel asked, then kicked herself. *Obviously.*

"I have the most experience," he said casually.

Rachel looked over at him again in the dim light of the car. He couldn't have been older than thirty.

"You don't look old enough to have the most experience," she said, earning her a slight smile.

"Age isn't everything. I've made up for my age by taking higher risk jobs that allowed me to gain more experience. I was recruited to Thomas Security a few months ago," he said.

"Recruited from where?" Rachel asked.

"From somewhere," he said with a mischievous grin.

Rachel raised an eyebrow. "Meaning they head-hunted you, correct?"

Reed met her gaze. "Thomas Security doesn't advertise positions. They network and recruit based on who *they* want. It's the only way to get in," he said.

"Sounds like the Illuminati," she said.

Reed raised his eyebrows and gave her an amused smile, not denying it. "The best move your king has made is hiring Thomas Security. People in our world are starting to talk, and soon that news is going to find its way back to his enemies. They'll be scared, and then they'll start making mistakes. That's when we'll make our move."

"How do you know they'll make mistakes?"

"Because it's hard to think straight when the boogeyman is behind you."

Rachel wanted to make a smart remark, but her brain was taking a time-out. She couldn't think properly when he looked at her like that—his arrogant smirk was hot as hell.

What is wrong with me?

She barely noticed when they pulled up at the palace, and then the realization jolted her.

How could she not realize she was at the palace? The palace! Rachel had never thought she'd step inside, let alone be living—albeit temporarily—inside it.

"What's in that file?" Reed asked as she shifted her bag on her lap.

"What file?" she asked, momentarily confused.

"The file in your bag," Reed said.

Rachel stopped—she'd forgotten about the file Abi had asked for.

"IFRT business," she said with a shrug.

He raised one eyebrow. "IFRT business is Thomas Security business now."

She raised an eyebrow in return. "You can speak to Abi about that."

"I will," he responded without pause.

Once they were safely inside the palace garage, the car doors unlocked and Reed said, "Please wait for a moment."

He stepped out of the car and reappeared at her door, opening it for her.

"Madame," he said, sounding like he was holding back a laugh. He walked beside her. "Abi's in her living room," Reed said.

Rachel tilted her head, wondering how he knew that. She supposed someone had let him know via his earpiece.

"Good to know," she said, heading there.

She knocked on the door and security answered, letting them in. Abi was sitting on the couch looking bored as hell.

"Hey," she said, lighting up when she saw Rachel. Her eyes immediately went to Reed and widened slightly.

"Reed, Abi. Abi, Reed," Rachel said, her voice still shaky.

Reed extended his hand to Abi.

"Pleased to meet you," Abi said.

"Likewise. I have a meeting, so I need to go. I'll see you later. Take care, Rachel," he said, his eyes lingering on her a moment before he turned and left.

Abi's eyes returned to Rachel, her lips turned up, and then she looked to security. "Can you give us a few minutes?"

They nodded and left the room.

"Who is he?" Abi asked, her voice a whisper.

Rachel knew security wasn't far away.

"One of Thomas Security's new recruits," Rachel said as casually as she could muster, but Abi clearly wasn't fooled.

"Interesting," Abi said with a smirk.

"You're telling me," Rachel said dryly. "This Thomas Security crew redefine bad boys. I mean, seriously, why are they all so hot? James, Deacon, even the nerd guy is hot! And now this ninja walks in with a smile that'll make your panties wet."

Abi tilted her head back, laughing. "The hot nerd guy is Samuel, for your reference."

Rachel shrugged, smiling. "Here's the file. Reed asked about it. You should read it quickly before they steal it," she said with a laugh, but she was deadly serious. "Where's Asher?"

"Working. He's been in his office all night," Abi said, her voice sounding far away. She returned her attention to Rachel. "He'll be fine," she said, perhaps more to herself than anything.

"What did you want this file for?" Rachel asked. She'd asked Abi that earlier and Abi had told her she'd tell her tonight.

Abi's eyes darted to the door security had left through.

Abi opened the file, flicking through the documents. "I keep having nightmares, Rachel. I'm talking in my sleep, saying, 'Don't touch me.' I wake up and feel like I should remember something, but I can't. And then I was sitting with Lenna this morning and I asked her to draw some memories of the times she wasn't sad." Abi looked at her. "She drew a man with a syringe in his hand."

Rachel frowned. "What?"

"Exactly. And then I thought . . . maybe they had a doctor there sedating women. I was only unconscious once during my captivity—I think, at least—and I felt the blow to my head before I lost consciousness. I woke up on the cell floor, bound again and numb. I assumed I'd only been out a short while, but now I'm not so sure."

"What does this file have to do with it?" Rachel asked.

"This case is one from before you joined IFRT. All of these captives reported memory loss, and all of them came from Adani."

"What are you saying, Abi? You think you were drugged? You think you were raped?" Rachel asked in a rush, her voice barely audible.

Abi shook her head. "Drugged, possibly. They could've injected me while I was under. I might've had a prick mark on my skin, but with everything that was going on I didn't notice. However, I don't think I was raped; I wasn't sore, and I haven't bled or had any discomfort."

"Right, so if you were drugged, what does it matter?" Rachel asked.

"Because I'm worried about how *heavily* I was drugged. If I was only lightly sedated, I could've been talking," she said in a hushed voice.

"Shit," Rachel said under her breath.

"Exactly. I could've told them anything—I could've told them exactly how IFRT operates, I could've told them things about my past . . ." she said, clearly pained.

"You don't know that happened," Rachel said quickly.

"My gut feeling is that something bad is going to come from it," Abi said, looking away.

Rachel took her hands. "You're alive and we're all back together. Whatever happens next, we deal with it together, right?"

"I'm worried about the fallout I'm going to bring on Asher, Rachel. He doesn't need me, he doesn't need—"

Rachel cut her off. "Asher is smart, and he makes his own decisions. He knows you don't have a clean past, even the security team knows that. If Asher wants you by his side, that's his decision to make. You're making a mountain out of this before you even know if there's an issue."

Abi nodded but Rachel knew she hadn't completely gotten through to her.

Rachel opened her mouth to continue when Reed walked in. "May I please have that file?"

Rachel looked to Abi, who looked defiant.

"I haven't reviewed it yet," she said, crossing her arms over her chest as if protecting it.

"I'll have it back to you within the hour," Reed said without pause.

"Once you've copied it?" Abi asked with a raised eyebrow.

Reed smiled cordially. "Exactly. File, please."

Abi held his gaze and Rachel watched the standoff between them. Eventually Abi passed over the file. "You have thirty minutes."

Reed raised an eyebrow. "Yes, boss."

He turned and left without another word.

"I don't like him," Abi said petulantly, sounding like a child.

"No, you don't like anyone telling you what to do. God help King Asher," Rachel said with a laugh that sounded more like a groan.

Abi chuckled. "Did you see the paper this morning?" she asked, her face growing somber.

"I did . . . They love Asher. They really do," Rachel said simply.

Abi sighed. "They're hailing him. That's great, for now, but people are fickle, and the higher they hold him, the farther he has to fall when they decide they don't like him again."

Rachel looked at Abi pointedly. "Do you believe in him?"

"Yes," Abi said without pause.

"Then push those worries from your mind," Rachel said. "Stand beside him, and keep him on the pedestal. Asher knows what he's doing, whether he thinks he's prepared or not—his father made him crown prince for a reason. His succession came sooner than intended, for sure, but sometimes the best way to learn to swim is to jump in. You're going to have to learn to let go, Abi. You're a planner, a controller, and that's why IFRT did so well during your tenure. But this is different—you need to let Asher lead."

"I think he's going to lead us to war," Abi said under her breath.

Rachel nodded. She had no love for war, but she didn't think there was an alternative, not this time. The King and Noah had been slain, and the Kingdom threatened. Asher had to retaliate.

"Then we'll get our guns and stand beside him," Rachel said.

REED

"James," Reed said, answering his phone as he strode toward the King's office. He'd memorized the palace floor plan on the flight to Santina—no small feat.

"You arrived just in time," James said.

"Tell me about it. It was a good call to head straight there," Reed said. James Thomas was one of the best strategists in the world, and every criminal knew it—that's why they feared him. "How's the interrogation going?"

"Slow. They're not talking yet, and they're out now. Hopefully they'll be feeling chatty when they wake up," James said. "Asher's ready to see you. Please do call him Asher, by the way. He doesn't want to be addressed as King Asher or His Majesty by us or anyone else. Jesse said he's never used titles with those close to him."

Because he doesn't have an ego, Reed noted.

"Copy," Reed said.

"Once you're done with Asher, I'm going to send you an address. I want you to check it out tonight. Take two teams. Be careful," James said.

"What am I looking for?" Reed asked.

"It's *who* you're looking for: Colonel Stevens," James responded. "I don't think they've moved him out of Santina yet, and I want to find him—dead or alive—before they do. Samuel has an address. It's a long shot, but at this stage it's all we have."

"Do you think he's alive?" Reed asked under his breath.

"I think we have about twenty-four hours to find him or we never will," James said, his voice urgent. "Samuel will send you the details once you're done with your meeting."

Reed refocused his mind. Right now he had a meeting with the king.

He entered the office that adjoined King Asher's office. Jesse was stationed by the door. "Reed," he said, remembering him from their very brief introduction earlier that day. "Asher is ready for you."

Reed nodded. "Thanks," he said before entering.

Asher looked up when Reed walked in, closing the door behind him.

Reed knew his age, and he'd seen many photos of Asher. But for some reason, seeing him at a desk that was clearly designed for a king was startling. He seemed too young, the role too heavy a burden.

But who was Reed to judge? Besides, he always loved seeing the underdog win.

"Asher, my name is Reed. I arrived earlier today and will be working closely with Jesse," Reed said, even though Asher already knew this.

"Thank you for coming. Please take a seat," Asher said, gesturing to the velvet seat opposite him.

Reed sat on the chair, immediately feeling uncomfortable. He never thought he'd walk inside a palace, let alone take a seat opposite a king. In fact, Reed had never thought he'd be so much as invited inside a palace. Reed had a temper, one that had almost ruined his life until he'd learned how to channel that anger. At sixteen, he'd started boxing, MMA, and he'd been good, really good. He was the best fighter on Thomas Security payroll—even James Thomas had never been able to beat him. Now all he needed to do was learn to control his mouth, Reed thought wryly, because he had an uncanny tendency to tell people to fuck off.

"James tells me you're in charge of the teams here," Asher said, his eyes narrow but not sharp.

"Correct. I'll be supervising them along with Jesse. Jesse is still in charge, but I'll make sure things run smoothly," Reed said.

Asher studied his eyes like he was looking for something. "And James will ask you to do things that he doesn't want Jesse to know about, right?"

Reed refrained from smiling. King Asher was no fool. "We do what needs to be done. Sometimes that involves testing people and sometimes that involves hard truths. But regardless, we do what is right, and what is needed—not what is easy."

Asher clasped his hands together, leaning forward slightly. "Tell me what you think about Colonel Stevens's kidnapping."

"I think the colonel was hiding something, with good intentions or not, and we'll know what that was shortly," Reed said.

Asher raised an eyebrow. "How is that?"

Reed was glad he'd asked. "We have a lead on an address where we think he's being held. I'll be heading there once I leave your office," Reed said, keeping his voice low. There was a risk that Thomas Security weren't the only ones who'd planted cameras in the palace. They'd done a sweep when the teams had arrived, but as the group had learned the hard way, some devices were very difficult to detect and could move constantly.

Asher studied him a moment. "I won't take up any more of your time," he said.

Reed stood, nodding. "Thank you. I'll keep you updated."

He turned to leave and as he did he noticed something on Asher's desk. He paused. "Where did you get that?" Reed asked, watching Asher carefully.

Asher frowned. "Get what?"

Reed pointed to the phone on his desk and then put a finger over his lips. Asher's eyebrows wove together.

"The pen," Reed said. "That's a very nice pen. And very expensive."

"It was a gift," Asher said without missing a beat.

Reed picked up the cell phone that had caught his attention. Reed knew Asher would've been given a Thomas Security phone, but the phone on his desk was different. All of their phones were marked with an "X," but this phone wasn't. Reed wouldn't have noticed except that the phone had been positioned screen down and the light cast by Asher's desk lamp made the back surface look like a glassy lake. It definitely wasn't marked in the same way. He ran his finger over the surface, but the phone didn't have a scratch.

It was new. Too new.

Reed grabbed a piece of paper and a pen and wrote, *Your phone has been switched. Don't say a word until I return. Don't touch the phone.*

"Very nice," Reed said. "I might have to get myself one of those. I'd better get going. I'll talk to you soon."

"Thank you. Keep me posted," Asher said, watching him carefully.

Reed called Samuel the minute he was out of the office and away from potential listening ears.

"Samuel, we have a problem. Asher's phone has been switched—he's not using one of ours."

"What?" Samuel asked quickly. "I'm monitoring the feed. He's using our phone."

"Well, the phone on his desk doesn't have the Thomas Security mark," Reed insisted.

"That's impossible," Samuel said, but the conviction in his voice faded with each syllable. "I need you to get me that phone. I'll loop some sound footage into our system so anyone listening doesn't suspect that we know."

"Okay. But I also just told him about Colonel Stevens," Reed said.

"One thing at a time," Samuel said, his voice calm. Reed could hear his fingers tapping on his keyboard. "Okay, footage is linked. Grab that phone, go to your room, then call me."

"Copy," Reed said, turning on his heels.

He walked back to the office and gave Jesse an apologetic nod. "Sorry, I forgot something."

Jesse knocked and then opened the door. Asher threw a wary look his way. Reed closed the door behind him quietly and brought his fingers to his lip again. Reed didn't know who was listening or how they were listening, and he wasn't prepared to take any chances.

He picked up the phone, slipped it into his pocket and left again.

Reed watched everything and everyone on the walk back to his new living quarters but no one was paying him much attention. In his bedroom he messaged Samuel: *I have it.*

Take the SIM card out and put it in your eDisk.

Reed pulled out the slimline kit he always carried in his back pocket. He pulled out the pin and ejected the SIM card and then slid it into the eDisk—a thin piece of plastic that was one of Samuel's inventions.

Reed's phone rang.

"Samuel," he said, answering the call.

"Okay, I've looped in this phone too, so the people on the other end don't know we know. I've traced it back to an address I'm sending to your phone now. James is in the office with me and he wants you to go straight there. In the meantime, we'll work out who switched Asher's phone, because it could only have been someone close to him."

"Copy," Reed said. "What do you want me to do with the phone?"

"Put it in the bathroom cabinet and leave it there until instructed otherwise," Samuel said as Reed's phone beeped, indicating a message had arrived. He looked at the address and then clicked on the map icon. It was a twenty-minute drive at most.

"I'm on it," Reed said, grabbing a full kit. He threw it over his shoulder and headed for the garage.

He passed Jesse again in the hallway.

"Going somewhere?" Jesse asked, clearly not missing Reed's pace.

"I'll be back in ten," Reed said vaguely. Ten hours, perhaps, but definitely not in ten minutes.

Jesse gave a disapproving nod. He didn't like being kept in the dark, and Reed didn't blame him. Jesse had been running security for years and now the dynamics were changing. But Jesse had requested their help and this was how they worked. It had always amused Reed that most of Thomas Security clients didn't like working with them—they hated the lack of control and briefings—but they knew Thomas Security got the job done, and so they dealt with it. *Smart people do.*

Reed felt eyes on his back, but he kept walking.

Asher's phone had been switched, and Jesse was the prime suspect.

ASHER

Asher looked over the financial reports, massaging his neck as he did. A large payment had been received from the Adani government yesterday as per the aid deal Asher had brokered, but today it felt like blood money.

A knock at the door pulled his attention and William Bennett entered. "May I?" he asked.

Asher nodded. "Please take a seat," he said.

William sat opposite Asher with his hands clasped in his lap. He sighed. "I told Abi," he said, sounding drained.

"What did she say?" Asher asked gently.

He gave a weak smile. "What you said she would," he said. "I've carried that burden for so many years, always afraid my family would find out and hate me for it. If I'd known how good it would feel to be rid of my shame, I would've done it many years earlier. I have you to thank for that, Asher, because if you hadn't made the deal with your father and we hadn't had that conversation, I don't think I would ever have told Abi in particular. She has such high expectations of this world and everyone in it; I didn't want to disappoint her."

"Abi has a good heart and she was always going to forgive you," Asher said without hesitation.

William Bennett's eyes dropped to the file in Asher's hand.

"Financial reports," Asher said, pushing them aside.

William Bennett met his gaze. "How much are you short?"

Asher bit his lip. "Well, if I count Adani's aid payment, we'll break even this quarter."

"But you don't want to take it, do you?" William asked.

"I feel like I'm betraying my father by accepting it. And I'm also letting him down by not accepting it." Asher rubbed his tired eyes.

"How much is it?" William asked slowly.

"Two hundred million," Asher answered, eyeing the man. Asher had asked him if he would provide for Santina if Adani withdrew their support. But Adani hadn't—Asher just didn't want to take their money. Money wielded power, and the last thing Asher wanted or needed right now was Adani having any power over Santina.

"Send it back, then," he said like it was the simplest thing in the world. "I'll give you four hundred million—two hundred this quarter and two hundred the next. In the meantime, we'll work on strengthening your international ties, and you can build aid deals that way. Despite our feud, I truly thought your father was a great king, but I always thought he should've bolstered international ties, especially with America. Santina has been too reliant on our region for too long. I know you receive international aid, but the majority of it comes from our region. That needs to change."

"I agree," Asher said. Their region was important, but if Santina was going to survive, he needed to expand relations.

"Look, I can't teach you how to be king, but I can teach you how to be a good businessman, and how to become wealthy. Money doesn't buy happiness, but it sure does solve a lot of problems. And it gives you options—options like telling Adani to fuck off."

Asher smirked. "That would be nice." He paused then, regarding the older man frankly. "Are you doing this for Abi?"

William nodded. "Of course. If she's in this with you, I want her to succeed. But it's more than that—Santina is my home, and I want my home to flourish. If I could see Santina built into a powerful, wealthy kingdom in my lifetime and know I played some small part in that, it would make me very happy. I've conquered much in business and in all honesty, I've been a little bored lately. This would be a challenge, and I love a good challenge," he said with a smile.

"It's going to be one," Asher said, but he felt infinitely more confident now than he had ten minutes ago.

"Challenge builds character," he said, like it was a saying he told himself every day.

"Is that written on your mirror?" Asher asked with a cheeky grin.

William chuckled. "It might as well be. My father made all his children repeat it every morning over breakfast."

Asher smiled. "How many siblings do you have?" He thought William Bennett had two sisters, but he wasn't entirely sure.

"I have two younger sisters and a brother, but he passed away some time ago," he said, his eyes seeming far away.

"I'm sorry to hear that," Asher said.

William nodded. "He fell from a horse and broke his back. It was tragic, and such a waste."

Asher nodded. He couldn't imagine it, but he could sympathize with William's grief—it was like a phantom that always seemed to loom nearby.

Asher's phone rang and he answered it.

"It's James. Keep Bennett talking—ask as many questions as you can."

"Thank you," Asher said before ending the call.

"Apologies for the interruption," Asher said, and William nodded. "What do your sisters do?" he asked. He was interested, and he was fulfilling James's request.

"One is a lawyer—she comes in handy," he joked. "And one is a cardiac surgeon—hopefully I'll never need her services."

Asher smiled. "All high achievers, then. Perhaps we should tell all Santinian fathers to make their children repeat your father's motto over breakfast."

William laughed. "They'll think you're some whacko, Asher."

"I'm not concerned with what they think," he said, surprising himself with how true that was. "My father told me that when he closed his eyes, he needed to be able to sleep with his decisions. I never fully understood the gravity of that until now. If I'm making good decisions for Santina, that should keep most of the criticism at bay." Asher wasn't delusional to think he would ever please everyone, but he would never make a decision he couldn't live with.

"Smart move," William said. "I figure you have a few weeks of praise yet until the vultures start wanting a piece of your skin." He stood. "I have an early morning meeting, so I'll leave you to it, but I'll arrange for the payment to be made tomorrow. You have my word," he said, extending his hand.

Asher stood, shaking it. "Thank you."

He was alone again and the first thing he did was telephone James Thomas. "Is there an issue with him?" he asked quickly.

"Not at this stage, and we just verified everything he told you. He has an interest in Santina, and the wealthier Santina becomes, the wealthier he will become—but that's not a bad thing. We will continue to monitor him; however, he's done nothing to raise any suspicion, and we've done a full audit of his financials. There's nothing unusual there," James said.

Asher's eyebrows lifted. "Exactly how much is William Bennett worth?"

"Sixteen billion USD," James said. "He's possibly the richest man in the region, and one of the least well known billionaires. Sure, he moves in influential circles, but he keeps a very low profile—he doesn't seek fame, at least not outside Santina. We like him, even more so that he just funded your Kingdom. We were going to offer you the money, so he took care of that for us."

Asher's jaw fell open. "You were going to offer it?"

James chuckled. "Well, as a deal of sorts."

"You have that much?" Asher asked, suddenly terrified of the bill that was due to come for Thomas Security services.

"I can obtain that much," James said.

Asher paused, and then decided he didn't want to know.

"Let's refocus," James said. "I'm going to show you a picture of

Henry Walker." The television on his wall activated and a photograph flashed up. "Does he look familiar?"

Asher studied the man's face, but it was the people in the background who stole his attention. "No, but when was that photo taken?"

"Six months ago. Why?" James asked, his voice seeping with curiosity.

"Because the third person to the right, with his back to the camera, is Noah," Asher said, his voice almost a whisper.

Judging by the slight pause, Asher knew James Thomas hadn't worked that out.

"You can't see his face, Asher. Are you sure?" James asked.

"I'm certain, that's absolutely Noah," Asher said. "Can you zoom in on the image? Noah had a mole behind his right ear. I don't know if you'll be able to . . ." His voice trailed off as the image magnified and the resolution adjusted. Suddenly, the mole was clear to all.

"Well, that might change things," James said at length.

"Noah wasn't mixed up in this," Asher said quickly. Noah wasn't here to defend himself, and he wasn't going to let his late brother's name be dragged through the mud.

"I wasn't immediately implying that, it just gives us another angle to look at," James said. "Do you know who the guy next to him is?"

"Yes, it's my cousin, Troy," Asher said. The side profile of Troy's face could be seen and he looked to be talking to Noah. Nothing there seemed out of place, except that Asher couldn't think of when this would've been taken—or where.

"Where was this taken?" Asher asked more specifically.

"At the last speech your father gave at the town hall," James responded.

"I would've been standing beside Alistair," Asher said absentmindedly as he tried to recall memories from the day.

"Asher, I'm going to show you another image—one we obtained from another angle," James said.

The image flashed up on the screen and Asher ground his teeth together. Noah was facing the camera, and there was fury in his eyes.

"He's not happy," Asher said, wondering what would've elicited that response from Noah—the happiest guy Asher had ever known.

"And then there's this," James said.

The image changed again, but this time the field was wider. Asher frowned, scanning the crowd, looking for the reason James was showing him this image.

When he saw it, he knew.

Colonel Stevens was in the picture, and he seemed to be staring at Noah. He didn't look pleased.

Suddenly Asher felt ill. Had Noah known something? Asher had always believed Noah's murderer had thought he was Asher and had needed to tie up loose ends. It hadn't occurred to Asher that Noah was in trouble because he knew something he shouldn't have. But why wouldn't Noah have told Asher?

They had told each other everything . . . or so Asher had thought.

REED

"I have eyes on the building. No movement as yet," Samuel said through his earpiece.

Reed kept his foot on the accelerator. He was a few minutes from his destination and he could feel the adrenaline running through his veins.

"Records show the apartment was leased three months ago to a company. A shell company," Samuel continued.

"Which means we're on the right track," Reed said. Shell companies were often used to hide other companies or financial maneuvers.

"Possibly," James said and Reed wondered at what point he'd been connected in. His voice was calm, and without a hint of urgency.

Reed on the other hand was riled up, ready for battle.

"I think you should move in straight away," James said. "There's a chance they've worked out the phone has been identified and we're already too late. We can't see movement on the CCTV footage, but it's possible we've missed something."

"Copy," Reed said, pleased by the news—he had no desire to sit around and scope out a building.

His eyes flickered to the rearview mirror. Clear.

"We'll be observing. Watch your back," James said.

"Got it, boss," Reed said with a hint of a smile.

He parked his car a few blocks from the apartment and strolled casually in its direction. He wore sunglasses and a baseball cap. He had a low profile in the criminal world, but every minute spent working with Thomas Security seemed to be raising that profile.

His eyes darted to the windows, looking for drawn curtains—or curtains just wide enough to peer through. He looked at the pedestrians passing him by, noticing if one of them looked a second too long. But he noticed nothing unusual, and that was either a good thing, or a very bad thing—it could mean he was too late.

"Reed, the apartment is a complex with two small courtyards. We think it'll be best to enter the courtyard on the ground floor and then scale three levels via the rear courtyard. You'll be much less visible and have the element of surprise," James said.

"Sure thing," he said dryly, hoping like hell he could scale three levels. He could do it if there were appropriate finger holds, but he wasn't Spiderman. Nothing about working at Thomas Security was easy, though, and he hadn't been hired to take the easy option.

He saw an elderly lady approaching the apartment complex door. He rushed forward, conveniently helping her with the door.

"Thank you so much," she said in a frail voice. "There are very few gentlemen left in this world."

Reed refrained from chuckling at the irony—she had the wrong idea about him. Of all things Reed had ever been called, "gentleman" wasn't one of them.

"After you," he said, giving his most charming smile.

He closed the door behind them.

"Straight ahead, fourth door on your right," Samuel said.

Thomas Security's intelligence support was unparalleled.

He walked ahead with the confidence of a man who had walked these corridors many times before.

"Excuse me," the old lady called out from behind him.

Reed paused, making a concerted effort to hide his irritation. He really hoped he wasn't going to have to silence her.

"Yes?" Reed responded casually.

"I didn't catch your name," she said with a smile.

"Luca," he replied without missing a beat.

"Nice to meet you, Luca," she said. "Can I ask a favor? Would you mind—?"

Her cell phone rang, interrupting her—and while Reed might not be Spiderman, his Spidey senses were tingling.

"Get out of there," James urged.

"I'm sorry, I have to go," he said. As he turned he saw her wave dismissively as she concentrated on finding her cell phone in her handbag.

Reed continued to the door as instructed. He felt eyes on him and turned to see the lady talking to another man.

The man's gaze lifted to Reed's, and Reed didn't like what he saw.

"Keep moving," James said.

Reed saw the courtyard to his right through the floor-to-ceiling glass windows and he exited through the door. He didn't look over his shoulder again, but he felt eyes watching him.

In the courtyard, Reed ran to the closest column and jumped, his fingers catching the adjoining lattice. He hauled his body up with a grunt and swung his legs over the balcony as he heard the door open.

Reed flattened his back against the column as he peered down.

It was the same man who had been talking to the old woman.

Reed sucked in a breath and stayed as still as a statue. The man's footsteps echoed through the courtyard as he moved. By the pattern of his movement, Reed deducted he was looking for something, or someone—almost certainly Reed.

Reed continued to stand tall and silent. The footsteps didn't continue but unless the man had taken off his shoes, he hadn't retreated into the building.

He counted the seconds, waiting until a few minutes had passed before he dared to take another look. He inched forward, doing his best to stay concealed behind the column.

He leaned over, scanning the empty courtyard.

What the fuck?

The man was gone.

Reed's head snapped side to side, scanning the balcony, but he saw no threat. He looked down again, but the man definitely wasn't there. Reed hadn't heard him leave, though, so where was he hiding?

Reed didn't know, but he knew he couldn't stay hidden behind the column any longer.

He crouched down and crawled forward, making sure he was covered by the vine that was growing on the balcony lattice.

His spine tingled and every nerve in his body fired. His instincts told him something wasn't right, but he didn't know what it was.

Reed moved as fast as he could while he kept low. He was at the end of the balcony when he dared to look down again. He saw the man standing underneath the balcony, the sleeve of his shirt sticking out from behind the column.

The man was exactly underneath where Reed had been hiding.

"James, I've been spotted," Reed said in a hushed voice as he saw the man draw a weapon. "He thinks I'm still behind the column."

Reed's call to move had been the best decision he'd made in a long time.

"Do you have a clear shot?" James asked—just as a shot fired. "Yes," Reed said, drawing his weapon. Now that a shot had been fired, all bets were off and the element of surprise was gone. There was no point playing nice now. Reed fired three shots—hitting the man in the back twice, and once in the base of his skull. Blood sprayed over the white column and the man fell.

Reed didn't hesitate. He scaled the lattice and jumped for the balcony railing of the higher level. The adrenaline coursing through his veins made the jump easy, and he swung his legs over, ducking behind the vine while he listened. He could hear voices in the courtyard, a scream, and then someone shouting for an ambulance.

Too late for that.

He looked left, then right. He needed to go up one more level, but with so many people in the courtyard, that was going to be impossible. He needed to go back inside the building.

"Apartment 2B is a two-story townhouse," Samuel said, reading his mind.

Genius, he thought.

Reed stayed low as he ran toward 2B. He knocked on the door and said a silent prayer when no one answered. He pulled a round disc from his kit and placed it on the lock. He waited a few seconds and then tested the handle. The door opened, and he found himself marveling at yet another of Samuel's inventions.

He closed the door behind him and ran for the stairs, taking them two at a time. He listened for any movement, but the house was silent.

He unlocked the window and climbed out onto the balcony. He quickly realized this was a free-standing balcony and unlike the lower levels, the balcony didn't lap the courtyard.

He peered over the balcony to the ground below. The crowd had dispersed—likely told to leave—while paramedics were placing the man on the stretcher. They weren't making any attempts to revive him.

"Any movement?" Reed asked as he did his own surveillance. Samuel had told him to run to 2B because it was a townhouse, and because it neighbored the apartment Reed needed to get inside.

"*No movement*," Samuel said.

"Reed—*go*," James ordered.

REED

*R*eed drew a deep breath as he took a few steps backward. Then he sprinted the short length of the balcony and hurdled over the railing, catching the neighboring balcony. He swung hard, crashing into the balcony footings. He winced as his hip hit the concrete but he knew he didn't have a second to waste.

With a deep breath, he hauled himself up and landed on the balcony like a cat. The doors opened and Reed stood with his pistol pointed. The man's eyes doubled in size as he came to a halt.

Someone inside spoke a language Reed didn't understand. The voice was calm, but Reed could tell the moment they realized they had a guest.

People inside began shouting and Reed charged forward, grabbing the man who had walked through the doors. He put up a fight and Reed narrowly missed a job to the cheek, but he was no match for Reed. Reed landed one blow to the man's nose and a lighter one to his cheek; within seconds he had him subdued. That was his goal—Reed could kill a man with a punch, but that wasn't his aim, not right now.

Reed brought his pistol to the man's temple. "Now you'll find out how loyal your friends are," he said in the man's ear.

He fought again, but Reed's iron grip was relentless.

Inside the apartment, Reed's eyes swept over the setup and straightaway knew this was a temporary control center of sorts, and he'd need to move fast if he wanted answers. The man's friends had already proved how loyal they were—they'd run, leaving behind their friend.

Reed tightened his arm around the man's neck, fighting against him until he went limp. He could hear voices below, and the fact that they hadn't left the building told Reed they didn't want to leave anything behind.

He sprinted in the direction of the voices, which were becoming more frantic by the second. A man ran out of a room directly in front of him, and Reed fired his pistol without hesitation, hitting the man in the leg. He howled as he fell and Reed delivered a lethal shot to his chest—his goal might not be to kill, but he wasn't stupid, and he wasn't letting that guy get back up. A door behind him slammed and Reed turned, his weapon poised. He crept forward, his eyes checking the open rooms as he did. Each room was a mess, but not the kind of mess that resulted from a ransacking. It was the kind of mess that told Reed they'd been stationed there for weeks, likely months. This setup wasn't recent. He noted the bland white walls and stained gray carpet.

He paused at the door he'd heard slam. He heard muffled voices, but he couldn't make out what was being said. Something sounded like it was being dragged and Reed's pulse hitched. He kicked the door open before whatever piece of furniture they were dragging blocked him out. Bullets greeted him and hit the hallway wall across from the door.

Reed pulled a mirror from his pocket and angled it into the open door. The apartment grew silent, and Reed knew they were waiting for him to make a move. He stayed still.

Eventually, he saw the tiniest of movements and knew where one of them was hiding—behind the bookcase. A pistol aimed in Reed's direction and he knew he had to move. He dove across the open door, firing at the bookcase. The gunfire that returned was deafening and Reed guessed there were at least five men inside the room. And these men weren't going to run—they were planning to fight.

"*Reed?*" James asked urgently.

"Copy. Just making some new friends," he joked as he grabbed a robot from his kit.

He swore he heard James chuckle.

"*I'm in,*" Samuel said as the robot began to move. "*Put them all down.*"

Reed had four robots in his kit and he placed them all on the ground. They drove off in all directions and Reed wondered how many men Samuel had controlling the little things.

He shook his head.

Focus.

He wasn't out of this alive yet, and he still didn't know what they were trying to hide.

Reed stood, pressing his back against the wall.

"*Four men. Two o'clock, four o'clock, six o'clock, ten o'clock,*" Samuel told him.

"Do I have clear shots?" Reed asked, drawing another weapon.

A pause followed before Samuel said, "*You've had worse odds.*"

Reed took a calming breath, and then with two steady fingers on the triggers of his pistols he stepped inside, firing blind in the directions Samuel had noted.

A few bullets were returned in his direction but their aim was off, hitting the walls next to him. Reed fired again, over and over, until he was sure they were dead.

"Why would they come into this room?" Reed asked, as much to himself as to James and Samuel. "They put themselves in a dead end when they could've run out of the apartment."

"They were protecting something," James said quickly. "Find it."

Reed ran to the bookcase and pulled out the books, looking for anything unusual—a book that was lighter than it should've been, or a book that was concealing a secret cavity of some kind. He cleared the shelves but didn't find anything. Reed ran to the desk and rummaged through the drawers.

"*Reed, you have company. Seven men are coming up the stairs,*" Samuel warned.

"How long do I have?" he asked without pausing. He opened the next drawer and searched it.

"A few minutes at best," Samuel said.

Reed looked over the room. He didn't have enough time. Not even close.

He felt defeated . . . and then his eyes landed on something.

Reed moved toward the slouched man and grabbed his wrist, taking a better look at the watch.

It could be a coincidence, but he knew not to trust that anything was.

"Reed, you need to move!" James urged.

Reed quickly undid the watch and turned it over, looking at the inscription.

"He's wearing the colonel's watch," Reed whispered.

"What?" James asked.

"The watch on this guy's wrist. These guys are linked to the colonel—and the only ones alive and able to talk are those coming up the stairs, along with the guy I met on the balcony," Reed said.

"There's nine of them," James warned.

"And if they shoot like these pansies I won't have any trouble," Reed responded.

He waited for a moment, but James didn't command him to leave. Reed reloaded his weapons in the few seconds he had left.

He tucked the watch into his pocket and hid behind the door. He heard voices as they entered the apartment, but Reed had no plans to let them find him.

He peered into the hallway and one by one they entered. He waited until he had a clear shot at three of them and then fired. They fell to the floor and, as expected, the others charged in. Reed hit two more before he had to retreat.

He pulled a flashbang from his backpack and threw it into the hallway. The second he heard it go off he charged forward, firing blindly. Three more fell.

But where was the last man?

Reed paused, his heartbeat the only sound in the room. His heart was beating so hard he thought it was going to bruise his ribs.

"Samuel, where's the other man?" Reed asked as he heard the faint sound of sirens.

"Last room on the right. I followed him, but I can't get the robot underneath the door," Samuel said quickly.

"Copy," Reed said, creeping forward cautiously. His weapon was up and he was poised to shoot—or fight hand to hand.

He was at the door when he heard, "It's done."

A sick feeling swelled in his stomach as he kicked open the door.

The man inside held his arms up in surrender. He wore an arrogant smirk. "You're too late," he said, his eyes darting to the left.

Reed followed his gaze and his stomach sank, churning violently when he saw Colonel Stevens bound to his chair, his throat recently slit.

ASHER

Asher clicked through the files on Noah's computer, and each time he opened a document he felt like he was betraying Noah by doubting him. Thomas Security had searched the computer, but they wanted Asher to look again—he might see something they might've overlooked.

He opened file after file, but nothing seemed out of place. Asher opened the photos application and his heart was bombarded with memories he'd forgotten. Asher's childhood flashed before him one click after another. All of Noah's and Asher's birthdays, photos from family trips and random miscellaneous photos. Asher clicked through them, laughing despite his breaking heart when he saw one of Noah dressed as a chicken for Halloween. How his mother had ever thought that a good costume, he wasn't sure. Hot tears pricked his eyes—it was a bittersweet memory. He made a mental note to ask Samuel to transfer all of these photographs to his computer.

As Asher continued looking through them, he noticed how few there were of Alistair. Noah and Alistair had never been good friends, but Asher didn't think there had been malice between them. However, looking at the photos, it was like Alistair had never existed.

Asher paused on that for a minute, but continued on. Part of him wanted to linger on the photos of innocent, happier times, and the other part of him wanted to lock them away in a part of his memory he couldn't access—somewhere they couldn't break his heart over and over again.

Asher closed a folder and opened a new one. He frowned. They were of a young woman and a baby boy; he couldn't have been more than a year old. Asher stared at him. There was something familiar about him, but Asher didn't know why he'd think that—Noah didn't have any children, and this kid didn't look like Noah. But there was something about him . . .

He called Samuel, who answered on the first ring.

"Samuel, I'm looking at Noah's computer and there are some photographs of a woman and young boy. I don't know who they are."

"Just a second . . . I see," Samuel said, and Asher assumed Samuel was logged into Noah's computer now. His assumptions were confirmed when the images started changing, flicking from one to the next until they'd looked through the entire file. "I'll run her face through our facial recognition software and see if we can find out who she is. It might take a few hours or so to get a match—there's a huge amount of data for the program to search through."

"Sure," Asher said. "Can you copy everything from Noah's computer to mine? I want to keep a copy of his photographs."

"Of course," Samuel said without a pause. Asher thought it would probably take him no more than a minute to do.

"What's your gut feeling on Noah?" Asher asked.

He didn't know what he'd do if Noah had been involved in this mess. Noah had always been his closest friend—the person he trusted most in the world. If that turned out to be a lie, Asher didn't know how he'd ever trust anyone again.

"I wanted to show you another image, actually," Samuel said and Asher didn't miss that he'd deflected the question.

An image flashed up on Noah's computer. It looked similar to the ones Asher had been shown before, but there was one major difference.

"The colonel . . . He seems to be looking past Noah," Asher said.

"I agree," Samuel said. "From the angle we showed you previously, it looked like he was looking directly at him, but now I'm not so sure," he said thoughtfully. "Now that we can see his eyes are going to the left, maybe he wasn't looking at Noah at all."

Asher frowned. "Show me the images of the crowd again," Asher said and they flashed up on his screen. He looked over the faces, looking for anyone he recognized—especially those in line with the colonel's gaze—but the angle wasn't good, and a lot of the faces were turned in the other direction.

"I can't get an image showing their faces," Samuel said, voicing Asher's own frustrations.

Asher leaned forward, scrutinizing the crowd. He took his time, silently naming people he recognized. He stopped on a woman with long dark hair. He couldn't see her face, but her hair matched. "Samuel, is that her? The picture of the woman with the little boy. Her hair matches," Asher said, but his confidence faded as he spoke the words. A lot of women in Santina had long dark hair. His mind was frayed, his nerves were frayed, and he was suspicious of everyone.

Samuel paused. "Impossible to say. But if I can obtain an identification match for her, I might be able to track her to the town hall and then follow her through the crowd. Let me work on this."

"Thank you," Asher said, his eyes lingering on the woman. It was just a photograph, but Asher felt uneasy looking at her. His wariness wasn't helped by the fact that she was standing next to Noah.

"The interrogation of the men captured at IFRT is about to start," Samuel said, pulling Asher from his thoughts. "Would you still like to watch?"

"Please," Asher said, and the screen changed again. Footage of the cell flashed up on his screen and two men sat opposite each other.

One was bound, one held a knife.

Asher leaned back, crossing his arms.

"Who sent you?" the man holding the knife asked.

The other man rolled his eyes.

Asher cringed as the knife slammed into the other man's thigh. He howled, cursing a string of profanities.

"I can do this all day. You cannot. Tell me who sent you."

His voice was menacing and it gave Asher the chills. He could only imagine what it would be like to sit in front of that man, bound to a chair. James had informed Asher the agent who would conduct the interrogation was one of their best, and he'd be able to get answers. Watching the footage, Asher wasn't doubting that.

The bound man's lips snarled up. Asher didn't think he was ready to give in.

"I'd rather die," the man said.

"Okay," the agent said before he slammed the knife into the man's arm. Asher sat back like he'd been jolted with an electric pole. His eyes narrowed at the knife, wondering how many anatomy classes this agent had taken. The knife was buried deep in the forearm, indicating he hadn't hit bone, and it didn't look like he'd hit an artery. At least blood wasn't gushing out when the knife was withdrawn.

The man was alive, but he was screeching so violently Asher turned down the audio on the computer for a second. When the man looked calmer—almost like he was going to faint—Asher turned up the volume again.

"Who sent you?" the agent repeated.

"You'll never find him," the man said breathlessly.

"On the contrary. I am going to, and you're going to help me do so," the agent said, pulling something out of his back pocket. Asher squinted to see what he was holding. Pliers, Asher realized.

"I don't know! I don't know who he is!" the bound man said quickly. He'd obviously come to the same conclusion as Asher about how those pliers were going to be used.

"How do you communicate with him?" the agent asked.

"Telephone," the man said in a rush. "Only telephone."

"So you take telephone orders from a man you've never met? That's not very smart."

"The others vouch for him."

"Who are the others?" the agent asked, sounding like he was losing patience.

"104Raiders. They all said he's the next leader of Santina. They vouch for him and threaten anyone who doesn't support him," the man said, as his fear of the man in front of him outweighed that of these 104Raiders.

"Who is the next leader?" the agent asked.

The man hesitated and the agent grabbed his bound wrists from his lap and pulled one finger toward him.

"Martin! Martin Snider!" the man said, hysterically.

Asher stilled—Martin Snider was the man who had helped Alistair broker the deal.

"I'm working on it, Asher," Samuel's voice came through the computer speaker.

Asher's mind was reeling. "Find out about the group he named," Asher instructed.

He wondered if they were a radical group, a group from Adani, or a Santinian military unit, because he knew their units named themselves.

"Working on it," Samuel repeated. "I'll update you when I find something."

"Thank you," Asher said, feeling more unsettled than ever.

Santina is bleeding from the artery.

Asher had a horrible feeling that a poison was spreading through his kingdom.

Was it too late to stop it?

Or had the damage already been done?

ABI

Abi stared at the mirror, barely recognizing the woman staring back at her. She smoothed out her dress, hoping it wouldn't crease as she sat. She stretched out her arms, checking the sleeve length, but the tailor had hemmed the sleeves perfectly. She turned on the side, noting the way the simple black dress hung perfectly.

After today, there would be no more hiding in the shadows for Abi. Her methods of distancing herself from her family were over. After the funeral, she would be Abigail Bennett, girlfriend of King Asher.

She suppressed a shiver. She didn't like media attention; she had loved living quietly, doing her own thing with IFRT, but that life had ended when she'd been kidnapped. She could never successfully run IFRT now. One of the reasons IFRT had worked so well was that Abi had kept the balance right. They attracted just enough attention to be considered important enough for people, like the men they bribed, to work with them—but not so important that they garnered a lot of attention.

The moment she was kidnapped and her family name was released, all of that had been jeopardized—and when she was identified as Prince Asher's girlfriend, every last ember of hope was smothered.

IFRT had to find a way to exist without Abi as its leader.

And she had to find a way to live without it.

Her reflection stared back at her.

Asher was right: she would be able to help more people than she ever could have if she carried the title of queen.

She straightened her shoulders and fixed a loose lock of hair that had escaped the bun at the base of her neck.

A knock at the door startled her, but when she saw Asher enter, she immediately relaxed. He looked striking in a crisp black suit, and for a moment she forgot to breathe.

"How are you feeling?" he asked, seeming to study her.

"Weird, to be honest. I've always escaped the media, and now I'm about to walk into the brightest spotlight I've ever seen," she said. Her voice was a little shaky and Asher didn't miss it. He gave an understanding nod as he took her hands.

"We'll do this together. If it makes you feel any better, I don't love the spotlight either, but you do get used to it in a sense. Speaking of, I have something for you," he said, holding out a small box.

She hadn't noticed him holding it, and now she couldn't look away.

"What is it?" she asked.

He gave a small smile. "It's a gift from my mother—a loan for today. You need to return it after the service, but she would like you to wear it."

"Okay," she said, but there was no conviction in her words. Asher didn't miss it and he tilted her chin up so she was looking directly at him.

He brought his lips to hers and kissed her gently, taking her breath away for the second time in minutes.

"I will always take care of you, Abi. And today doesn't change anything—if you decide, at any time, that you want to walk away from this life, from us—you can," Asher said with a low voice.

Abi exhaled, melting into his arms. "I want to be by your side, I was just . . . freaking out for a moment," she said with a forced smile. She was *still* freaking out a little.

Asher pulled back, giving her an odd grin. "Then you're really going to freak out now," he said as he picked up the box again and opened the lid.

Abi sucked in a breath. She knew the custom, but she didn't expect to be included in it, not today of all days.

Even in the dim bedroom lighting, the emeralds and diamonds sparkled bright. "It's beautiful," Abi managed, her voice a throaty whisper.

"My father gave it to my mother for the first official event she attended. She would like you to wear it today, but it's your decision."

It was tradition for members of the royal family to wear a tiara or headpiece to all official events. Despite not caring a whole lot about fashion, Abi had always admired Queen Emilia's sense of style, and this tiara was no exception.

Asher looked at her expectantly. She realized she hadn't responded.

She nodded hastily, needing to pull herself together. It was like someone had kidnapped her mind this morning. Where had brave Abi gone?

Asher placed the tiara on her head and turned her to face the mirror. He stood behind her, a full head taller despite the fact that she was tall herself. Carefully, no doubt wary of her back, he wrapped his arms around her waist, threading his fingers through hers. She took that moment to take it all in, and Asher seemed to be doing the same.

He closed his eyes, kissing the crown of her head, letting his lips linger. "I'm scared too," he said, barely audible. "But things are going to get better."

Asher's eyes were still closed, but the conviction in his words was unmistakable. Her nerves faded, and with them her hesitation. Abi had always done everything alone—she'd had team members at IFRT, of course, but she'd carried the weight and responsibility of their decisions.

But she didn't have to carry the burden alone anymore.

They would carry Santina's burdens together.

She felt the tension melt from her shoulders, and maybe it was a coincidence, or maybe Asher felt it too, because he lifted his eyes, meeting hers in the mirror. She gave a small nod and he smiled.

"You look amazing," he whispered in her ear before planting a sweet kiss on her neck.

Abi heard voices outside the bedroom door and knew it was time.

With her hand in Asher's, he led her out of the bedroom and toward the garage. She recognized Emilia immediately, her dancer-like posture impossible to miss. What surprised her, though, was that her parents were standing beside her.

Abi looked to Asher, but he didn't seem surprised.

"You and I will walk together, and your parents will walk with my mother," Asher said.

Abi paused. "Where is Alistair?"

"Alistair won't be attending," Asher said without missing a beat, but his voice made her stop. She looked at him and he shook his head. "Later," he said as Abi's mother turned, seeing them.

"Oh my," she said, her eyes on Abi's tiara before landing on Emilia.

Emilia turned to face them. Her eyes softened as she looked at Asher and then she smiled when she saw Abi. Emilia wore her hair down, but the bandage on her neck was clearly visible—something Abi didn't think was an oversight.

Emilia's eyes darted between Abi and Asher and she smiled. Asher kissed his mother's cheek before shaking her parent's hands. Abi's father and Asher stepped aside, seeming to have a quiet word. Abi was focused on them until Emilia stole her attention.

"It suits you. You wear it well, Abi," Emilia said.

"Thank you, and thank you for thinking of me today. I can't imagine how hard today is going to be for you, and yet you still managed to think of this and gave the tiara to Asher," Abi said, squeezing her hand.

Emilia squeezed her hand in return and her eyes were wet. "Don't make me cry. I've already ruined my makeup twice this morning, and if I have to ask my aid to do it again she's going to resign," Emilia said weakly.

Abi pulled a tissue from her purse and handed it to Emilia to dab her eyes. "Thank you," she said.

"Are we ready?" a voice beside her asked. Abi looked up to see those black eyes that seemed even more unreal now he was standing in front of her. "Nice to finally meet you in person, Abi," James Thomas said, extending his hand. "Let's get everyone into the cars," he continued, looking past Abi.

Abi had so many questions for him, but security swept in, guiding them into two different vehicles.

Abi slid in next to Asher and he took her hand, placing it in his lap. James Thomas took the front seat, and it took her a moment to realize Deacon Thomas was in the driver's seat. She'd only seen him once during the first videoconference call they'd had, but she was sure it was him.

The A-team had been brought in for today, and that helped settle her nerves.

"Hello, Abi," Deacon said.

She assumed Asher had met them all this morning, or perhaps even last night. She had no idea when they'd arrived.

"Hello, Deacon," she said, letting him know she remembered him.

The corner of his lips turned up but his attention returned to the road. As they approached the palace gate, Abi sucked in a breath and lowered her gaze. There must've been hundreds of reporters with huge cameras waiting for them. Asher ran his thumb over her knuckles and she was momentarily distracted. He was used to this as much as someone ever could be, but he was aware enough to realize she wasn't.

Once they were past the reporters and heading toward the church, Asher leaned in, close to her ear. "It's going to be worse at the church. Focus on me and stay by my side. Don't let go of my hand," he whispered as he kissed her cheek.

"Okay," Abi said, steeling herself.

"At the cathedral, Asher," James said, turning to face them, "you and Abi will enter first, and your mother and the Bennetts will follow. Security is lining the walls of the cathedral, and Deacon and I will walk beside you and Abi. As we previously discussed, this is not a discreet strategy—we don't want to be discreet. We want everyone watching you to know that you've tightened security, and we want them to know *who* your security team is. We want them to squash whatever plans they currently have of making you their next target," James said, his eyes on Asher.

"We have snipers on every rooftop surrounding the cathedral, and snipers inside. Today, your focus is on the service and your speech. Let us handle the rest," James said, full of confidence.

"Be the man on the balcony," Asher said.

Abi's eyebrows wove together. What man on the balcony?

But James Thomas must've understood, because he gave a knowing smile.

"Exactly," James said, and Asher drew a deep breath.

The drive to the cathedral seemed to be taking forever, and it took Abi a few wrong turns to realize it was a security strategy. As was said, they weren't going to take the most direct route—security was taking a scenic tour through Santina instead, keeping anyone with sinister plans guessing.

But even if Abi hadn't known the streets of Santina, she would've been able to guess when they were close to the cathedral because the streets were lined with people. She'd never seen so many Santinians gathered in one area.

She took a calming breath. This was a new kind of pressure for her—a new challenge—and that's how she needed to look at it. She would not be weak, not now. She had more fight in her than she'd ever thought and she would not shy away from anything—or anyone.

Abi looked to Asher, and the only sign that he was stressed was his bouncing knee. His face was composed—like a mask of strength—but Abi knew it wasn't a mask. Asher, too, had more fight in him than he knew.

The car came to a stop at the front of the cathedral.

"Don't answer any questions. Don't say a word. Just keep moving forward. We need to get you inside quickly," James instructed.

Abi looked in the rearview mirror to see a second car behind them.

James turned to Asher. "Ready?"

"Ready," Asher said with a strong voice.

A flutter of nerves erupted in her stomach as the Thomas brothers stepped out of the car.

Asher exited next and was escorted around the car. He opened the door for Abi and she heard a flurry of noise as she stepped out: the unmistakable sound of camera shutters.

Asher took her hand, steadying her.

Abi heard what sounded like amplified hushed whispers—she supposed that happened when the crowd was all whispering the same thing.

King Asher has a girlfriend.

Security stepped in and once again they were surrounded by guards and swept forward into the cathedral.

Abi's breath hitched in her throat, but the level of coordination provided by Thomas Security was impressive, and they entered the cathedral without incident. They stood at the door as Emilia and her parents assembled behind them. Abi heard the organs playing inside, and it was only then that she felt a slight tremble in Asher's hand.

He was walking into his father's funeral, and Abi could tell the reality of that had only now just hit him.

ASHER

He had to actively fight the urge to run far away from it all, but this was his responsibility, and he had to face it. He dreaded the doors opening and seeing his father's casket. He remembered the moment he'd seen Noah's casket and he'd felt sick. Now he had to do it all over again.

Except this time he had Abi by his side.

Jesse appeared at his right—he'd been traveling in the car with Asher's mother.

"You can do this," he said under his breath. "Focus on anything but the casket. Keep your gaze straight ahead."

Asher nodded. Whatever Thomas Security thought about Jesse, they were wrong. Asher didn't doubt him—he'd always been there for them, and he'd always tried to bring out the best in Asher. If he wanted Santina to fall, he wouldn't have stopped Asher from reaching for that bottle. It might seem a small thing, but Asher knew something had shifted inside him that night, and he had Jesse to thank for that.

"Thank you," Asher said.

"Martin would be proud of you," Jesse said quietly, and Asher almost crumbled.

The doors opened and the crowd inside the church turned their heads for the first view of the royal family. Asher took a step forward, then another. His father's casket was covered in flowers, but there was no mistaking it was a casket.

The whispers started, as Asher knew they would, and he squeezed Abi's hand. This was a lot for a first appearance, and Asher now wished for the things he'd once resented—a date captured by the paparazzi. He'd thought that was bad, but this was next level.

But to her credit, despite everything he knew she must be feeling, she stood tall and confident beside him.

James Thomas took a step forward and Asher followed. He couldn't believe he was at a second funeral within as many months.

His eyes swept over the guests as they walked down the aisle toward the front of the cathedral. As they neared the altar, Asher saw the faces of dignitaries and diplomats his father had befriended. He nodded to a few as he passed by. When Asher saw the Adani king and crown prince, he fought to remain calm. He would not show them how much their presence affected him. But even if he hadn't been able to control his emotions, he realized it wouldn't have mattered—they weren't looking at Asher. Their eyes were on the Thomas brothers, and Asher knew they didn't like what they saw.

Asher held back a smile now. If his father could see them, he'd have enjoyed this.

Eventually the Adani royals did look to Asher.

Asher held their gaze. He didn't flinch. He didn't look away.

I'm going to ruin you, Asher thought, surprising himself with his newfound confidence.

The last place he'd expected a moment of clarity was at his arrival at his father's funeral, but perhaps his father was here, guiding him, because suddenly Asher knew how to retaliate. He wouldn't go to war —because he wasn't going to start a fight he couldn't finish. Instead, he would strip them of everything they loved and needed, just like they'd tried to do to him, and he'd show the world who they really were.

Asher returned his attention to the front. The sight of his father's casket only strengthened his resolve.

They were seated in the front row and Asher wished he could see where the Adani royals were looking now.

"You're filming everyone in here, right?" he asked in a hushed whisper.

"Of course," James said casually.

The priest entered and they stood.

The funeral followed traditional protocol, and Asher stared straight ahead. His gaze dropped to the casket and he drew in a shaky breath. Abi squeezed his hand and gave the slightest of nods. He pictured his father's slain body inside the casket and struggled to keep his emotions in check.

He knew he wouldn't be able to give the speech he needed to give in that state of mind, so he focused on something else: revenge.

"King Asher will now give King Martin's obituary," the priest said.

Asher stood and walked toward the podium. His notes were in the pocket of his jacket, but like he'd done with the speech on the balcony, he decided in this moment not to give his prepared speech. Not today.

Today, he would give a very different speech.

Asher's hands trembled and he drew a steadying breath. He looked at his mother—at the bandage on her neck—and at Abi, who was sitting slightly forward, because she couldn't lean against her chair, and then at the Adani royals. Their eyes connected for a moment and Asher knew that was all he needed.

"I thank every guest, every friend, and every Santinian for coming today to bid farewell to the greatest man I have ever known," Asher said, looking over the guests. "You knew him as King Martin; I was honored to know him as my father and mentor. In preparing today's obituary, I asked myself what my father would want me to say. I think he would want me to speak not of him—because despite his title he didn't enjoy the spotlight—but of his legacy."

Asher was flying by the seat of his pants now and he took encouragement from the nodding heads in the crowd.

"My father, King Martin, was a man of honor. He made hard decisions over easy ones, and he taught me that nothing is more important than family. He considered Santina—all twenty-five million of us

—his big family. He loved Santina and, more than anything, he wanted to see Santina flourish. That moment was stolen from him the day he was assassinated by those who pretend to be our *friends*," Asher said harshly, and a stillness settled over the cathedral. It was like no one dared to breathe.

Asher's eyes dropped to James Thomas, whose eyes shone with approval.

Asher continued. "But perhaps what those *friends* never knew about my father was that he was a brilliant chess player. He played anonymously online in international competitions, and until his death he was undefeated by all, except one person."

Asher looked to the Adani royals.

"That person is me," he said, and had the satisfaction of seeing their eyes widen.

Asher returned his attention to the crowd and looked into the cameras. "King Martin has departed for the heavens, but he is not gone. I will carry on his legacy and see his dreams fulfilled. When you think of King Martin, I ask you to think not of his tragic death. Remember him for the wonderful man that he was—a father of Santina."

Asher returned to his prepared speech now that he'd made his point, and when Asher spoke, he looked into the camera, speaking directly to the Santinians lining the streets outside, because this service was ultimately for them. He read from his notes and told everyone of the man he had known.

"This is the King's final farewell. He loved you, Santina, and you will forever be with him," Asher said. He placed one hand on the casket and closed his eyes for the briefest of moments.

Goodbye, Father. I won't let you down.

When Asher returned to his chair, James whispered, "Nice speech."

"Did I take it too far?" Asher asked.

"No. It was perfect," James said, his words full of praise.

Asher sat restlessly through the rest of the service. He kept it together as a few of his father's allies spoke, but when his mother went to the altar to blow out the candle on his father's casket, Asher felt his composure crack. He could avenge his father, but it would never bring him back. His mother placed her hands on the casket and Asher could see she was fighting to keep it together. She looked up at Asher, and he gave her an encouraging nod, but he wasn't sure his expression was one of strength. She wiped her wet cheeks and returned to her chair.

The priest concluded the ceremony and they stood, following security to the rear of the cathedral. As guests began to file out, Asher shook their hands, accepted their condolences, and thanked them for coming. Asher had no idea how long it took for the cathedral to empty, but it felt like hours. Finally, the Adani royals approached Asher.

"Thank you for coming to pay your respects," Asher said, his voice neutral.

The Adani king extended his hand. "We are sorry for your loss, King Asher. We need to talk—I'll be in touch."

"You know where to reach me," Asher said, not reacting to him. He would never give that man that kind of power—he didn't deserve it.

The king seemed unsure of Asher's response, but he nodded and walked away.

Asher extended his hand to the Adani crown prince, resisting the urge to punch him in the face. He repeated the same empty words and they left without incident.

Emma Bennett accompanied his mother out, but William paused beside Asher. He smiled gracefully. "My wife was right about you—you were born to be king."

ABI

Abi stole a look at Asher, Santina's king. They'd all thought he'd simply go to war, but that speech had left them guessing. Asher was going to do something special, and even she didn't know what that something was.

She realized she was staring, and when he caught her, his eyes softened. He reached out for her hand and she had never been more proud to stand beside him. He held her hand tight as security blanketed them. Abi didn't know if she was imagining it or if security had truly tightened after Asher's speech, but she felt safe behind the human fortress.

While Asher was keeping people guessing, the security team wasn't. Abi saw the glances being cast in the direction of the Thomas brothers, and whether the guests knew who was handling security or not, the security team had made it clear: they were not to be messed with. James Thomas seemed to have a natural ability to appear confident and threatening all at once.

Abi wondered more than once if Lamberi was somehow watching. Did he have a network of spies inside Santina?

She hoped security had appeared confident and threatening

enough to discourage him, but she knew that was unlikely. In fact, it might even encourage Lamberi. Men like him enjoyed a challenge.

Abi couldn't see past the human wall of security but she felt the Santinian heat the moment they stepped out of the cathedral. It lasted only a moment before they were escorted into cars and they made their way to the private burial grounds.

Asher rested his head against the seat and sighed as the car drove away. He was still holding her hand, and he threaded their fingers together then turned to look at her.

"How are you feeling?" he asked, surprising her.

"Me? I'm fine. How are *you* feeling?" Abi asked. She hadn't done anything but stand there beside him.

"I'm glad that's done," he said, sounding far away. "I hope my father is cheering me on and not rolling in his casket."

Abi gave a small smile. "Your father never went to war, but that would've been the easy option. You said it yourself: he was a strong king because he made the hard decisions. You will be the same—you've proven that today. And you left Santina in awe."

"Awe?" Asher asked, raising his eyebrows. "Did you talk to them as we left the cathedral?" he joked.

"I didn't need to," Abi said confidently. "The cathedral was silent; you could've heard a pin drop. No one expected that speech, and it was everything it needed to be. Threatening without being a direct threat. It was powerful."

Asher rubbed his temples. "We'll see if you're right over the next few days. But as I was standing there, I knew I couldn't play it safe, and I also know I can't go to war. Yes, we have a military, but we don't have the money we need to go to war, and unrest will only cost us more. I need to be strategic about this and plan my revenge via other means. I won't start a fight I can't win."

"So play the game you can," Abi said, knowing Asher would do exactly that. The best move King Martin might've ever made was to make Asher the crown prince. Abi wondered again if he had any inkling, even a gut feeling, that his life had been in immediate danger before his death.

"I don't specialize in politics," James said, "but I second that—play the game you can win. Strategy is what wins every war; not ammunition, not manpower. With a good strategy, a small team can defeat even the most powerful. Santina might be the smallest kingdom, and the poorest, but that doesn't mean you can't win. I'm telling you now, the Adani royals are not strategists, because killing your father was the stupidest move they could've made."

Abi looked between James Thomas and Asher and noted a shift between them. She supposed James Thomas's reputation had a lot to do with it, but Asher seemed to genuinely respect and appreciate his advice, and that respect didn't seem one-sided.

They drove in silence to the burial grounds, and when they arrived Abi had to say Asher's name twice before he opened his eyes. Asher hadn't been sleeping well but she thought the emotional toll the day was taking on him was more likely the reason he'd fallen asleep. He awoke, rubbed his eyes, and then seemed to take a moment to collect himself. When security opened his door, King Asher stepped out.

Security opened Abi's door, but here, in the privacy of the family, Abi didn't need—or want—to make a statement with Asher. This service was for Asher and his mother. Abi hung back in the shadows as the priest said a final prayer, then laid flowers on the casket before King Martin was lowered into the ground. Abi placed a flower too, silently farewelling the late King and thanking him for his life of service.

She returned to the car, giving Asher and Emilia a moment alone. Her eyes welled with tears as she saw Emilia lean on the casket, her body shaking as she sobbed. Asher put one hand around her shoulders and held her. He was strong even when he didn't know how to be.

Abi looked away, feeling like she was invading their privacy.

James Thomas came to stand beside her.

"How did you feel during the service?" he asked casually.

"What do you mean?" Abi asked.

"How did being so close to the Adani royals make you feel? They were looking at you, but their expressions were impassive. It's hard to know what they were thinking," he said, seeming to search her eyes for answers.

Abi shrugged. "Honestly, I felt like everyone was staring at me, and I was trying not to focus on anyone in particular. I was aware of where they were seated and I deliberately didn't look in their direction. I didn't think King Martin's funeral was the place to make a scene. Asher had enough to deal with without worrying about me."

James nodded. "Lamberi was seen in Santina this morning, Abi. I sent a team out, but by the time they arrived, he was gone. He's keeping a low profile, and we're still trying to work out how he entered Santina, but someone with official clearance had to have let him in. More so now than ever, you need to listen and do everything we tell you."

Abi raised an eyebrow. "As I have been doing for the past week. I haven't left the palace."

"I have a weapon for you—I know you can shoot—and I want you to carry it at all times, even inside the palace. The palace is safe, but recent events have taught me that no building is impenetrable. It's a worst-case scenario, but it's a precaution I think we need to take. Extra security precautions have been set up at the palace, and I'm honestly not expecting trouble, but it would be foolish for our team not to consider it and have plans in place."

Abi frowned. "Does Asher know this?" She was surprised he hadn't said anything.

"He'll be briefed when we return. He had enough to deal with this morning, and I didn't want to add any unnecessary pressure," James said, his eyes returning to Asher.

"Did you see the face of the Adani royals when Asher was giving his speech?" Abi asked.

The corner of James's lips turned up.

"I didn't, but my team was watching. The Adani royals got the message," he said, sounding amused.

Asher strode toward them with his mother by his side. Emilia's gaze was cast down as she walked and Abi thought she'd appreciate a few moments alone with her son.

"Emilia, why don't you ride with Asher? I'll go with Jesse and Reed," Abi offered. She looked to James Thomas for approval. He paused, seeming to consider it, and then nodded and began escorting everyone into cars.

In the back of the sedan, Abi stretched out her legs and closed her eyes, but as soon as Lamberi's face flashed in her mind, she opened them, suddenly no longer tired.

She focused on the road ahead, grateful for a few minutes of silence. Jesse drove and Reed sat in the passenger seat. She studied him for a moment and paused when she saw what looked to be a bruise underneath his chin. She leaned forward.

"Yes?" he asked, eyeing her cautiously like she might attack him. Reed was a little high strung, something she'd thought the first time she'd met him.

"Why is your jaw bruised? It looks fresh," Abi remarked.

Reed raised a lazy eyebrow. "One of my guys caught my chin during a practice session."

"Huh," Abi said, but she wasn't sure she believed him. There was an underlying hint of something in his voice. Excitement? If it was, his tone didn't match his explanation.

Reed turned back to her. "How's your ankle? You hardly limped today."

"I'm dosed up on painkillers," Abi said, like it was a joke, but it was actually the truth. "I'm sure it's going to ache tonight, but it is much better. Hopefully another week of rest and I might start training with you. I want to learn how to throw a punch that leaves a bruise like that."

Reed chuckled. "God help the king."

"What's that supposed to mean?" Abi asked.

Reed smiled. "I meant it as a compliment, Abi." He didn't elaborate, and Abi let it go. She noticed Jesse hadn't said a word. His eyes were on the road.

She looked ahead and the light changed from red to green in perfect timing, such that Jesse didn't need to slow down—but then it happened again at the next light, and then the next.

"Good run with the lights," Abi noted.

Reed smirked. "The traffic fairies are on our side today."

But his smirk quickly faltered and Abi knew something had been communicated via the men's earpieces because their body language shifted in an instant.

"Copy," they said in unison, and Jesse pulled a hard left like it was a turn he hadn't been expecting to make. The car sped up and Abi held on to the armrest for support.

"Get down!" Reed shouted, a few moments before the back window shattered. Glass showered over Abi as she put her hands over her head for protection. Her head was on her knees and she didn't dare look up.

Her heart hammered against her chest and she felt like she was going to be sick. The car swerved again and shots were fired from their car—she assumed it was Reed, but she didn't dare look.

Do everything we tell you. James Thomas's words rang in her ear, and she kept her head down.

"Go! Go! Go!" Reed screamed as more shots were fired and another window was smashed. Abi didn't know if it was a side window or the front window now. How many people were firing at them? Were they being ambushed?

Was this how King Martin had felt before he died?

She shook her head, refusing to go there. There was a different security team in place—the best in the world—and they would handle it.

She heard a barrage of gunfire so loud it sounded like a thunderstorm.

"Stay down!" Reed shouted and Abi nodded when nothing came out of her throat. Fear had stolen her voice, and unlike when she was taken from her car and captured, this time she didn't know the procedure and what to expect, and that left her unprepared and asphyxiated with fear.

The car swerved so violently Abi fell to the side, banging her head on the door. A hand reached out, grabbing her—cushioning the fall.

More shots fired, coming from their car.

"Go!" Reed said, his voice slightly less urgent.

Abi stayed huddled down, counting the seconds so that she had some sense of time.

Where were they?

How long had they been under attack?

She'd never felt more useless in her life.

"Abi?" Reed asked. "Look at me. It's okay now."

She raised her head, her eyes landing on his bleeding arm. The front windshield was shattered, and in fact almost every window in the car was shattered except the one to her right. Abi was surprised she hadn't broken it with her head.

"What happened?" she asked, her voice raw.

"Are you okay?" he asked, looking over her as if searching for injuries.

"I think so," she said vaguely, sitting up. She twisted, looking behind her. She saw two more cars that looked like replicas of the one she was in.

"An attempted ambush," Reed said, not sugarcoating it. "This time we were more prepared." He placed a hand on Jesse's shoulder. "Nice driving, Jesse."

Jesse nodded. "You okay, Abi?"

"Yeah," she said, able to breathe again. Her heart was no longer like a marching band in her chest, and she could think again.

"Where's Asher's car?" Abi suddenly asked, panicked.

"They're ahead of us," Reed said. "He's fine."

Abi exhaled in relief, noting her shaking hands. She looked to them, as did Reed.

"You're in shock," he said. "We'll be at the palace in a few minutes."

"I left the cathedral in Asher's car," Abi said, trying to make sense of it all—no one should've known she'd switched cars.

"You might not have been the target," Reed said.

ASHER

Asher paced the garage, waiting for Abi's car to arrive. He didn't know whether to be livid with Thomas Security that the attack had even happened, or grateful that they'd been able to protect Abi. It had been a very different outcome than the ambush on his father's car.

When the garage door opened and he saw the car dented with bullet holes and barely a shard of glass left in its windows, his stomach churned violently. He rushed toward the car at the same time James Thomas did.

"Abi," Asher said, opening the door.

"Careful," James said, stepping in and helping Abi out.

"I'm okay," she said quickly, but the usual confidence in her voice was missing.

Asher pulled her into his arms and kissed the crown of her head. He held her tight because he was very aware the circumstances could've been very different.

Reed spoke quietly to James and Jesse, and they all seemed in agreement with whatever was being said. Asher wanted to know exactly what that was.

James noticed him watching them and walked over. "Let's get Abi inside and I'll brief you both."

They walked to Asher's office, and he noticed Abi was trembling slightly. "Take a seat," Asher said and went to the fridge to get her something to drink. He found some juice and sat beside her, holding her hand. He squeezed it tight, not knowing how he would've coped if something had happened to her.

James dragged a chair over and sat opposite. "Samuel is working on the footage now, so we'll have more information in a few hours, but essentially, this is what happened. Our car," he said, looking at Asher, "was a few minutes ahead. The first shot was fired at Abi's car as they turned onto Embassy Road. We had the maps planned out and I had snipers positioned on rooftops along every road we were mapped to take," James said, and Asher paused, impressed.

"The snipers took out the first car, but two more came from behind. Reed took out the driver of one of those cars and another sniper hit the other. There were three cars involved in the attack and five men in each car. We have a few of them in custody—the others were killed on site."

"How many men attacked my father's car?" Asher asked.

"Fifteen, three cars," James said, knowingly. "You and Abi left the cathedral together, so unless someone was able to witness the change of cars at the burial site—which would be extremely unlikely—Abi wasn't the target. Your mother was."

Asher sucked in a sharp breath. "Why?"

"She may be Queen Mother, but she still has influence over this kingdom. There's also the fact that your mother said she felt like she should remember something, but she can't. I think something was said, or maybe she recognized someone, and that person is attempting to tie up a loose end in case she does remember," James said.

"But no one knows my mother said that," Asher said, his mind reeling.

"But if she saw something, and they know it, they might just think it's a matter of time," James said. "Or maybe they do know because someone has leaked the fact that her memory is vague. We don't know for sure either way, and it's possible whoever is behind the attack didn't care if it was you, Abi, or your mother in the car. You're all targets."

"What happens now?" Asher asked, aware his voice was rising. He couldn't lose Abi or his mother. He couldn't.

"We interrogate the men and find out who sent them, and then we'll launch an attack. I know you don't want to hear this, but Abi's car being attacked and everyone surviving—including a few captives—was one of the best things that could've happened to this investigation. I'm not glad it happened, and I know it's traumatic for you and Abi, but it will open leads that might've otherwise taken months to develop."

Abi nodded, seeming to understand, but Asher didn't want to hear it.

"Make them talk," Asher commanded. "I want to know who was behind this attack."

A menacing grin formed on James's lips. "Making men talk is my specialty."

The look in his eyes was chilling, and it almost gave Asher the chills—almost.

His office phone rang, startling him.

"King Asher speaking," he answered.

"Your Majesty, this is King Khalil."

Asher raised an eyebrow. He had been expecting contact from the Adani royals, but not this quickly. He looked to James Thomas, who nodded. Asher frowned, wondering how he knew who was on the other line and then he realized his phone was monitored and likely someone had communicated via his earpiece.

"How can I help you, Your Majesty?" Asher asked, keeping his voice neutral.

"Your speech was quite a performance," King Khalil said. "And it seemed to be aimed at us. I don't appreciate false accusations being made, and certainly not voiced in such a public way. You forgot not to bite the hand that feeds you, King Asher. Adani has withdrawn all its aid," he said, sounding smug, which only infuriated Asher further.

"My speech was not a performance," he hissed, "and if you think you can dictate to me because you provide aid to Santina—you're very wrong. Yesterday I asked the bank to return your most recent aid payment. Santina will thrive without Adani's involvement," Asher finished bitterly.

He was met with only silence.

ABI

Where Was Prince Alistair?
Will Abigail Bennett Be Santina's Next Queen?
What Is King Asher's Next Move?

Abi scanned the newspaper articles as she sipped her coffee. Santina was rife with gossip this morning, as they'd all expected—and there would be even more when Santinians found out Asher had returned Adani's aid and refused to accept any further payments. She wondered what spin the Adani royals would put on that; she'd only heard Asher's end of the conversation, but she could tell it had been a terse conversation. He'd stayed in his office late and was gone from bed before she'd awoken. The only sign he'd slept a few hours was the crinkled sheets where he must've lain. She thought she vaguely remembered him drawing her into his arms, but she wasn't sure if that had been a dream.

"Good morning," his low voice said from behind her.

Asher wrapped his arms around her as he leaned over her shoulder. "What are you reading?"

"Gossip," she said, tilting her head back, finding his lips.

"I thought you said my father was torturing himself for reading the papers every morning, and now look at you," he said, searching her eyes, but she wasn't sure what he was looking for.

"Maybe I was wrong about that. It's important to know what the people are thinking, even if you don't agree with it. How else do you respond and connect with them?" Abi asked, as much to herself as to Asher.

He pulled out the chair beside her. "How are you feeling after yesterday? It was a long day, and a frightening one."

"Thomas Security handled it, and if anything, now I have even more confidence in them." She paused for a moment. "What do you think of Reed?"

"He seems competent, that's for sure," Asher said thoughtfully. "Honestly, though, I haven't dealt with him that much yet. My communication is mostly with James. Why do you ask? What do you think of him?" Asher asked, seeming genuinely interested.

"He's . . . interesting," Abi said slowly. "At times he seems a little high strung, but during the car attack he was as cool as a cucumber."

Asher smiled. "I think it takes a certain person to work security—you need people who perform best under pressure."

"It takes a certain person to be king too. I know this is never the role you wanted, Asher. But you're doing Santina proud. I'm proud of you," she said, looking deep into his eyes.

He cupped her cheek and brushed his lips over hers. "Thank you," he whispered, his voice deep and gruff. "I want to make Santina proud, my father proud. I want you to be proud—and proud to stand beside me."

Abi smiled. "You've already won me over, Asher. You did that before you were king."

He kissed her again and she melted into his arms. Her back was healing and had stopped bleeding through her bandages, and the cut on her lip was almost healed. She opened her mouth without wincing and kissed him properly for the first time in a long time.

"Abi," he moaned, kissing her harder. He grabbed her hips and drew her in. His forehead rested against hers. "The only time I forget about my role and the worries that come with it is when I'm with you.

For a moment, you steal my mind and release it from the prison of my title."

Abi tilted her head to the side slightly. "Do you really think it's a prison?"

"Sometimes, yes. At other times, it all seems manageable," he said thoughtfully.

"Do you know what I think?" she asked playfully.

The corner of Asher's lips turned up. "I think you're going to tell me."

Abi chuckled. "I think you put too much pressure on yourself. You said your father lived in the moment—in the present—and that's where you need to learn to live too. Yes, you need to plan ahead, but let tomorrow worry about tomorrow."

Asher's eyes dropped to the newspapers. He pushed one aside, revealing the paper with the full picture of them walking side by side. "Hmm," he said, his eyebrows weaving together.

Abi frowned. "You don't like the photograph?"

He shook his head. "No, it's not that. I like the photo, actually. But look at this person in the background," he said, pointing.

Abi's eyes followed his finger. She studied it for a moment, wondering where she'd seen him before. "That's the colonel's driver," Abi said quickly, thinking back to that dreaded night on the side of the highway.

"Captain Lewis Spencer," Asher said, sounding far away.

"Is it odd he attended?" Abi asked, unsure.

"Not really, but look at all of these pictures," Asher said, spreading out the newspapers. They were all similar photographs taken from slightly different angles—not surprising, given that security had allowed only one photo opp.

"His eyes are focused on you in all of them, and he's not smiling," Asher said.

Abi looked again. "Huh," she said, trying to make sense of it. The more she looked at the photographs, the more she didn't like it, but she couldn't exactly accuse this Captain Lewis of throwing daggers her way.

Asher returned his focus, perhaps having similar thoughts. "I'm untrusting of almost everyone," he said, looking pained.

"I have a good feeling about this security team," Abi said. "They're going to get to the bottom of this. When you know who you can trust, you'll be able to sleep at night."

Asher looked up as Abi heard footsteps beside her. James entered, making no apology for his interruption.

"Hello," he said, dragging a seat over to sit beside them.

"Hello," Asher said, picking up the newspaper. "Look into this guy—Captain Lewis Spencer. I don't like the way he's looking at Abi."

Abi watched James carefully. His eyes darted from one photograph to the next. "Okay," he said simply.

Abi frowned. "He's not exactly shooting daggers."

James shrugged. "Criminals usually aren't that obvious, and I've learned the hard way to trust your gut instincts. I admit I wouldn't have paid it much attention, but if you don't like it, Asher, we'll look into it."

Abi thought it was a waste of time, but supposed it couldn't hurt. Captain Spencer did know what happened that night and he could use it to his advantage if he had any malintent.

"He was there that night on the side of the highway," Abi said quietly, even though Asher already knew at least some of the details.

Now James perked up. "That might change things," he said, taking another look. He made a phone call. "Samuel, Captain Lewis Spencer. Run a full report for the past twelve months—I want to know everywhere he's been, who he's spoken to, and a full list of his assets. Thanks," he said before ending the call. James looked to Asher. "We'll have the information in a few hours."

Abi's jaw dropped open. "Doesn't that take more time?"

James smirked. "Not for Samuel. Now, the reason for my visit," he said, handing her a box. Abi opened it to reveal a small pistol. "Remember—keep it on you at all times. Take it even into the bathroom. I don't want to see you without it."

"Hang on, why are you giving her a weapon?" Asher asked, alarmed.

James's expression remained impassive. "I'm giving Abi a weapon because I know that no building in this world is impenetrable. Even my home was attacked once, and I thought I had every protection possible. I don't think it's likely that the palace would be attacked—if I did, I would've moved you out of here—but I won't take that risk. Abi knows how to shoot, so I'm giving her a pistol that I intend for her to never use. If you knew how to shoot, I'd give you one too. Given that you don't, a pistol will only be more harm than good."

"Perhaps you should teach me how," Asher said tersely.

"I'm planning on it, but not today. You have enough shit to deal with right now," James told him seriously. "There's one more thing you need to know: Lamberi is in Santina. I had an additional six teams fly in this morning, and my staff is on high alert. We don't know how Lamberi entered the country, but someone cleared him, and we'll find out who that was."

"How did you know?" Asher asked, his voice tight.

James crossed his arms like he was settling in for a long conversation. "We caught him on CCTV, but he's disappeared, gone underground, as we call it. There's a reason IFRT was never able to get a photo of him. He knows how to hide. We're good at finding ghosts, however, and in this world, with cameras on every street and communication devices monitoring every conversation, it's hard to hide for long."

Asher pinched the bridge of his nose. "Every time I think things can't get worse, they do."

"Actually, catching Lamberi on CCTV footage was a blessing. We don't know where he is, but we know he's close, and that's a good advantage to have."

Asher scoffed. "That's grasping at straws."

"In my world it's not," James said flatly. "Let me handle this. You stay beside Abi," he said, smirking now, "and she'll protect you with that pistol."

Asher raised an eyebrow. "Does your wife know how to shoot?"

James grinned and his eyes sparkled. "Of course she does. We have a weekly contest, but I still have the best shot—for now."

Asher gave a strained laugh. "You're a strange guy."

James chuckled properly now. "I've been called much worse things. Do yourself a favor and take the day off. You need some time off, Asher. Watch a movie or something," he said before turning to leave.

Asher smiled. "Let's go on an adventure."

"Within the palace?" Abi asked quickly.

A smile lit up his face. "Come with me," he said, standing and holding out his hand.

ASHER

*A*bi reached for his hand and he helped her up, making sure she was steady on her ankle. She took the pistol out of the box and tucked it into the back pocket of her jeans. Asher couldn't decide if he liked the idea of her having a pistol or not, but James was right: she knew how to shoot.

"How did you learn to use that?" Asher asked.

"I took self-defense and weapon training classes—a ton of them—after my mentor was murdered. I made all IFRT staff go through that training," she said with a sad smile.

Asher knew Rachel had agreed to take on the role of administering IFRT, but he wondered what would become of it without Abi's leadership. He knew it was hard for Abi to let it go too, even though she didn't feel like she had any other option.

He cupped her cheeks and placed a sweet kiss on her lips. "IFRT is going to survive," he said.

She looked up at him with troubled eyes. "We were just starting to make real progress." She looked away, shaking her head. "Those women don't have anyone else. Few groups will do the rescues IFRT was prepared to do. And I worry about Rachel . . . I love her, but I don't know if she has it in her. She always preferred more of a background role."

He didn't know Rachel well enough to say, but he knew one thing: "Sometimes we're pushed into situations that make us grow and become the people we're meant to be."

She sighed before looking up at him with a bittersweet smile. "You're right. I just—it's hard—I'm so used to controlling everything and right now I'm . . . I feel lost."

"You need something to work on," Asher said, nodding. "Luckily for you, Santina has a list of problems you can help solve. We'll talk about it tonight, but right now I want to show you something."

She beamed a smile and his chest warmed. It was like the night he'd taken her to the ruins—he loved her sense of adventure.

He led her into the hallway, walking slowly beside her, monitoring how badly she was limping. She seemed okay, so he continued on as security teams followed closely behind them.

As they approached the elevator, they filed in, jammed like sardines between security guards.

Asher was surprised to see security already in the tunnels when they stepped out into the underground level.

"What is this?" Abi asked as her head arced, taking in the series of tunnels that led out from the elevator.

"Secret passages," Asher said with a wink. "They were originally built to bring in supplies, and likely for people to come and go discreetly. They were closed off by my great-grandfather and restored when the palace underwent its latest renovations," he said as they walked. "As children Noah and I spent hours down here, exploring the tunnels and playing hide and seek."

His heart ached to think of Noah. He thought again of the image he'd been shown—the picture of an angry Noah that Asher couldn't reconcile—and wondered what had become of that lead. Asher supposed they were still working on it and focused on returning his attention to better times.

It had been a long time since they'd run carefree through the tunnels, but he could still remember the way Noah's laugh echoed through them, always giving him away.

"Did you ever get lost down here?" Abi asked, her eyes dancing.

Asher chuckled. "I don't know about lost, exactly, but there was more than one occasion when we'd spent a few more hours down here than intended." Despite the ache in his heart, it felt good to be in the tunnels and away from his office. He felt like Asher, not King Asher. Maybe that was why his father had always come down here.

"What are you thinking?" Abi asked gently.

Asher wasn't sure what his expression was, but his poker face was definitely not on, given the concern in Abi's eyes.

Asher shook his head. "My father built something down here a long time ago, before all the wars started and Santina was struggling. Some time ago he closed it down because it was a luxury that wasn't needed when our people were starving. It just occurred to me that was probably a bigger sacrifice than I realized, because I think it was his escape from the pressures of his title."

As they turned the corner, Asher saw his father's joy in the dark corner.

"Is that glass? What is that?" Abi asked, squinting.

"It was an aquarium," Asher said of the floor-to-ceiling glass structure built into the rock wall of the tunnel. "It was beautiful. It was lit up, bright blue, and was filled with colorful fish. My father had a big armchair down here and he would sit for hours. We used to watch him and laugh, thinking he'd lost his mind." Asher gave a guilty smile. "We would call him The Mad King. Now that I reflect on it, it was probably his form of meditation."

"It must've been amazing. It's enormous," she said, her head tilting up.

"But that was the problem, the cleaning and maintenance fees were exorbitant, and when the budgets were tight—or in the red—he couldn't justify his fish tank."

"Maybe one day it'll come back to life," Abi said with a genuine smile. She seemed to really believe that, and that meant she believed in Santina.

"Maybe one day," Asher said, knowing that if it did, that day was a long time from now. But maybe he could resurrect his father's pride and joy; maybe his own kids would call him The Mad King.

"What did the armchair look like?" Abi asked, her eyes still on the old aquarium.

"What?" Asher asked. "What color was it?"

"Yeah, what color was it? What shape?" she asked casually.

"It was blue velvet, like the chairs in his office. And it had a winged back," Asher said as a vivid memory of his father sitting in the chair flashed in his mind.

Abi squeezed his hand. "That's how you should remember your father."

"Sitting in his chair?" Asher asked, raising an eyebrow.

"Happy," she said, like it was the most obvious thing in the world.

He looked at the fish tank one last time before continuing his tour. He led Abi deeper into the tunnels, wishing security wasn't so close behind, but also grateful they were.

The walls were lit with small lights, so they didn't need flashlights, but still the tunnels were dark. Asher felt the same buzz feeding through his body that he'd felt as a kid.

"We're underneath the gardens now, near the palace entrance," he said.

Abi's head snapped to him. "Huh? I thought we were going in the other direction," she said with a laugh. "Don't leave me here, Asher, I'll never find my way out."

Asher laughed. "You should be on your best behavior then," he said as she swatted his shoulder.

"I am always on my best behavior. Angel Abigail is what they call me," she said, wiggling her eyebrows.

Asher laughed heartily. "Now that is the biggest lie I've heard in a long time."

Abi chuckled, but there was no humor in her voice. "No, seriously, they call me the Night Angel. She who comes in the night and rescues people."

Asher paused. He didn't know that. "The Night Angel . . ." he mused, drawing her in, wrapping his arms around her shoulders. "You're the bravest angel I know," he said quietly before he kissed her—not giving a thought to the security standing close by. If they were going to follow him everywhere, they'd better get used to it. Stolen moments like these with Abi would be rare, and he was going to take advantage of every single one of them.

"Excuse me, Asher," Reed said.

Asher pulled back, annoyed, before he realized that Reed hadn't initially been with them. When had he come down to the tunnels?

"Yes," Asher said, his tone sharper than intended.

"You need to look at something. Now," he said unapologetically.

Asher cleared his throat. "What is it?"

Reed paused for a moment, like he was debating telling Asher here in the tunnels. "We've picked up communication about a terrorist attack on Santina. James wants to speak to you immediately."

His stomach churned violently and he turned, striding toward the elevator.

It took him a moment to realize Abi wasn't beside him. He turned back, seeing her walking with security. She motioned for him to go ahead without her as she hobbled along.

"Do we know the timing for this attack?" Asher asked as Reed strode beside him.

"Imminent. James deployed teams to the site a minute ago," Reed said.

"You're not going?" Asher asked, not sure if that was a good thing or not.

"No, James and I are staying at the palace. This could be a legitimate attack, or it could be a setup to get us out of the palace and away from you. We're not prepared to take that chance. The deployed teams can handle it," Reed said.

Asher nodded, pressing the elevator button with more force than necessary. The doors opened.

"What communication did you intercept, precisely?" Asher asked.

"I don't know," Reed admitted. "I'd actually just arrived in the tunnels to relieve one of the security guards when the instruction came from James to bring you up. I'll be briefed at the same time as you."

Asher nodded. The elevator seemed to be moving impossibly slow but he was sure it was just in his mind.

He all but ran to his office.

James was there with the television on, and Asher could see Samuel and Deacon there, ready.

James started talking the second they entered.

"As Reed has informed you, we have intercepted communication regarding a series of terrorist attacks planned for Santina. We've verified the recordings and I've deployed teams to the sites involved, but we can't be sure if this is a setup as yet."

"How many sites?" Asher asked, feeling the acrid bile rise in his throat.

"Three. Town Hall, a subway station, and Rainbow Street—restaurant district," he said.

"Oh God," Asher said quickly, pacing. "We're talking about thousands of casualties."

"If the data we have is correct, we still have a few hours until the bombs are detonated," Samuel said.

"How long, exactly?" Asher demanded.

"Eight hours. I've identified six individuals involved," Samuel said, and then hesitated. "But the fact that I've been able to do that concerns me."

"How so?" Asher asked, his mind reeling.

"Because it's almost like they wanted us to know. They made careless mistakes—mistakes criminals below their pay grade would make," Samuel said.

Asher looked to James, and he knew he wasn't going to like what was said next.

"My gut feeling is that this is going to be a blackmail attempt," James said, seeming to choose his words carefully.

"Blackmail? For what? What do they think Santina has that's worth anything of value?" Asher asked, his mind going to Alistair's deal. "The oil well," he said, answering his own question.

"Possibly," James said, but Asher knew by the tone of his voice he didn't believe it was that.

"Then what?" Asher demanded.

James looked past Asher, to the closed door.

"It's potentially *who* you have, not what you have," James said, seeming to tense for his reaction.

It took a moment for the realization to hit him. And when it did, he felt like he had when Abi had sleepily punched him in the throat.

"No!" Asher said, his voice a wheeze.

James nodded. "It's the perfect storm, Asher. If I were Lamberi, I'd make this move too. If he blackmails you, and you refuse to hand over Abi, he'll initiate the attacks. If there are casualties, he will tell Santina you chose to save Abi instead of—potentially—thousands of innocent Santinians."

Asher pressed his fingers to his temple. "I can't . . . I can't . . ." He didn't even know what he was saying. He couldn't think past Lamberi's name.

"You don't have to do this. We will," James said, calmly. But Asher wanted him to scream—to be as furiously mad as he was.

"What are you going to do?" Asher demanded, his voice sharp.

"The first thing we need to do is wait for contact from Lamberi—if that's going to happen at all. Second, we need to continue to collect intel on the identified individuals. If we can find them before they attack, we can stop them and foil his plans. Third, we need to consult with Abi."

"Why?" Asher asked.

"Because we might need her to play a role in this," James said as Asher's eyes flared.

"In what way?" Asher all but shouted.

"That depends," James replied calmly. "Not as bait, but she might be able to play a role that will help you resolve this. If that's a possibility, it needs to be considered because if those attacks occur and you're blamed for them, you're going to be crucified."

"I'm not involving her in this. I'd rather be crucified," Asher said flatly.

James nodded but the determination didn't leave his eyes. "Let's wait and see what happens next. If contact is going to come, it'll come soon."

"How do you know that?" Asher asked.

James looked him dead in the eye. "Because I have the ability to think like a criminal without indulging in the behavior. That's why I'm a strategist—I can put myself in their shoes and predict their next moves. Lamberi has a single focus, and that makes him predictable."

"You knew he was going to do this," Asher realized.

James nodded slowly. "I thought it was highly possible, but I wasn't going to worry you until it eventuated."

Asher glared at the man. "What *else* have you not told me?" he hissed.

"I've told you everything you need to know," James said, his voice still damnably calm. "I won't tell you every bad thing that could happen because, frankly, I don't have the time, and it will serve no purpose but to make you lose your mind," James continued, his words contrasting starkly with Asher's unraveling thoughts.

"If you think this is blackmail, why have you already deployed teams?" Asher asked, reaching for the million questions in his muddy mind.

"At this point, they're there for intelligence purposes. They're looking for anyone scoping the area, anyone placing objects that could be bombs, or anyone looking suspicious in general. We can do that via CCTV, but we might miss something, so it's better if I have teams on site. These guys are what I call ghosts. They blend in and they're extremely hard to spot. Lamberi's guys won't see them—that's one thing I can guarantee."

James must've seen the doubt in Asher's eyes, because what James asked next blew his mind. "Have you seen two additional security teams following you around? Did you see them at the burial grounds?"

"I have multiple teams on me," Asher said slowly.

James shook his head. "These teams are in the background, at a distance. They hide in the shadows like ghosts, hence the name.

They're not there for bodyguard services, they're there to look for unusual activity your bodyguards might miss—someone peeking out from behind a curtain in a three-story-high building, someone walking a little too slowly or too fast. The ghosts are chosen because they have eyes like a hawk. They're on site now, and if there's something to see, they'll see it."

Asher felt some of the anger leave his body, but he was still reeling. He'd almost lost Abi once, and there was no way he was letting her leave the palace—if that's what was intended.

"We're going to wait for contact," James said, holding up a hand. "Once that's done, we'll make our plan."

RACHEL

"Abi?" Rachel called, spotting Abi walking jerkily ahead, surrounded by her security team.

Abi turned, giving a forced smile. "I was just looking for you."

"What's up?" Rachel asked, not waiting for a response. "You shouldn't be walking on that ankle. You're really limping again."

"It's fine," Abi said, waving her hand dismissively. As Rachel walked toward her she could see something was amiss. She knew Abi well enough to know when she was stressed.

"What's up?" she asked again, but Abi's eyes darted to her security team.

Rachel got the message.

"I need to go through some matters concerning IFRT with you. Let's go to your living quarters," Rachel said, knowing that was as much privacy as they were going to get.

As they walked past Asher's office, Rachel noted Abi looked at the closed door of the adjoining office. She heard low, muffled voices—like someone was yelling inside—and Rachel slowed her pace without thinking, but security was quick to hurry them along. She realized Abi had done the same.

In the living room, Abi asked, "Can you please give us a moment?"

Security nodded and left, although Rachel knew they were still being monitored via cameras.

"Are you okay?" Rachel asked as they sat on the sofa.

"I don't know," Abi said quietly. "Something big is going on. Reed escorted Asher to Asher's office—something to do with a terrorist attack. That was Asher yelling as we walked by," she explained, running a hand through her hair.

Rachel's eyebrows wove together—she hadn't heard the voices clear enough to distinguish who they'd belonged to, let alone what had been said. She tried to stay positive. "Well, whatever it is, they'll handle it," Rachel said.

Abi nodded but she seemed less confident. "Do you really need to talk about IFRT, or was that just a cover?"

Rachel smiled but there was nothing behind it. "You said you wanted to be kept updated, which I still think is a mistake—you're only torturing yourself by knowing things you can't do anything about."

Abi looked at her expectantly and Rachel sighed. "Three villages were attacked last night. That makes a total of fifty-one in the past few weeks. Other groups are stepping up their efforts, but everyone is afraid. They're saying if IFRT pulls out of the region, it will convince others it's too dangerous and they'll give up too."

"We're not pulling out! We're on forced vacation," Abi said, her words dripping with contempt.

"I told you this was a bad idea," Rachel said, pointedly.

Abi held her hands up in surrender. "I'm sorry, I'm not trying to take out my frustration on you. This whole thing is a mess, and I keep asking myself if I should've done something differently when I knew I was going to be taken. Maybe I should've run . . ." Her voice trailed off and she looked away.

"If you'd run, they would've put five bullets in your back," Rachel said without pause. "Don't blame yourself for this. You have given years of your life to IFRT and always put it first. You didn't ask to be kidnapped."

"It doesn't change anything," Abi said through gritted teeth. She stared at her feet, and then her head snapped to Rachel. "Tell them we're back. Tell them we'll have two teams on the ground tomorrow."

Rachel's jaw dropped into her lap. "Are you out of your mind? Who is going to lead these two teams? You're not, and I'm not allowed to leave either. I never thought I'd say this, but I'm beginning to dislike being confined to a palace."

Abi smiled. "You ungrateful princess," she said with a strained laugh. Abi and Rachel had always been able to find the humor in the darkest of situations—one of many reasons they'd survived in IFRT. "IFRT needs to have a presence right now. We can't let everything we've worked for be destroyed overnight. If the other groups are looking at us for leadership, we need to step up. Daniel's not confined and he can lead one team, at least. Maybe we can ask Samuel to help? With their intelligence, our missions would be a hell of a lot easier."

Rachel tilted her head thoughtfully. That was a damn good idea, but she didn't think James Thomas would be willing to extend his services that far. She didn't even know how Asher was footing the current bill.

Then again, IFRT did have some money if they could get him to agree.

"I really don't want to distract Samuel right now, though," Abi said with much less enthusiasm than she had moments ago. "He needs to be focused on Asher and finding his father's—and Noah's—killers."

"Agreed. But maybe there's something else we can do," Rachel said as an idea began to formulate in her mind.

But the idea remained only a seed, because Asher strode in, slamming the door behind him. He nodded as he bypassed them, going straight into the bedroom.

Rachel's stomach churned. Had Asher overheard them talking about sending two IFRT teams out?

"Um . . ." Abi said, her voice trailing off.

"It's okay, I'm going to make a few calls," Rachel said quickly. "I'll be in the guest wing with Lenna if you need me." She felt ill—the last thing she wanted was to cause trouble for Asher and Abi.

She gave Abi a hug and then nodded at security, who were

lingering in the adjoining kitchen. A few of them followed her out, but she understandably had a much smaller team than Abi or Asher.

She heard voices in the hallway. "My job is not to please Asher. It *is* to make sure he stays alive, and that Santina doesn't fall."

Rachel slowed down, but security didn't give her a chance to eavesdrop. Once again she had no idea who the voice belonged to.

"Twenty-four twelve," one of the guards said and with a gentle nudge she quickened her pace. When they turned the corner, the hallway was empty. Rachel knew she wasn't supposed to overhear that conversation, and now she second-guessed why Asher was in such a mood. She didn't wish a crisis upon him, but she would be relieved if he wasn't upset about IFRT plans.

She realized that despite living in the palace, she really didn't know what Asher was dealing with behind the scenes and what was being done about Adani officials. She knew she was being unfair to herself, but once again she questioned if she had the strength and courage she would need to lead IFRT. Abi was a good strategist, and that was one of the main reasons they'd been successful. Rachel doubted herself. Had she spent enough time in the palace, surrounded by security and daily encounters with the king, that she should know what was going on? Even an inkling? Had she missed things she should've paid attention to?

Not any more, Rachel decided.

From now on, she was going to treat this like a game. She wouldn't bemoan her confinement in the beautiful palace—because there were much worse places to be confined. And if she was surrounded by a team that was said to be the best in the world, this was her chance to learn.

That chance came much sooner than expected when Reed opened her door half a second after he'd knocked.

Rachel looked to her security team, who either weren't surprised to see him or were used to him entering as he pleased.

"Hello?" Rachel said, pointedly.

"Sorry for the interruption," he said with a straight face, but there was no apology in his voice. He'd said that purely for pleasantries, Rachel knew.

"How can I help you?" Rachel asked.

That question seemed to catch Reed off guard but then he shook his head, as if clearing a thought from his mind.

"I do need your help, actually," Reed said. "Well, Abi needs your help."

"Abi? What's wrong?" Rachel asked quickly.

"Take a seat," he said, his calm manner surprising her.

"Where is she?" Rachel said as panic rose in her throat like acid.

Reed, obviously noting her reaction, held out his palm like it was a stop sign. "She's okay, for now. Please, take a seat." He sat on the sofa and Rachel sat obligingly, knowing it was the only way she was going to get any information.

But she sat a safe distance—at arm's reach—which was hard to do given the small sofa, which was really more of a day bed.

Reed was too good looking, and little butterflies formed in her stomach whenever she saw him. She hadn't felt like this since Noah, she realized absently.

"We have a situation," he said, looking directly at her. "Asher is being blackmailed. Lamberi wants Abi, and if Asher doesn't hand her over, Lamberi is going to target seven heavily populated sites in Santina."

Rachel's stomach was in her throat. "Hang on—what do you mean, target?"

"Bombs. Likely suicide bombers," Reed said simply.

Rachel pressed her fingers to her temples as her head spun. "Oh, shit," she said, her voice a harsh whisper. "That's why he was so mad."

"Partly," Reed said. "Asher is more mad about what happened next."

Rachel's head snapped up. *It gets worse?*

"This is a difficult situation," Reed said, his eyes softening. Rachel wondered if it was a weak apology for what he was going to say next. "We have designed a plan, one which Asher doesn't like, but we think it's his best chance at beating Lamberi and, without trying to sound arrogant, this is what we do. Asher plays political games; we play security games. They are two very different skill sets and ways of thinking."

"What do you want me to do?" Rachel asked, her stomach churning.

Reed met her gaze. "We want you and Abi to go into Santina. We'll choose the location—one which gives us an advantage. We need to make it look like you're there on your own. We want Lamberi to find you both so we'll make that easy for him. I—and *multiple* teams—will be close by, but if any of us are seen, he'll know it's a setup. Abi can't go on her own, as that would look suspicious given her relationship with Asher. Lamberi would never believe she's walking around on her own."

Rachel frowned. "He's not going to believe it just because I'm there, either. Anyone who's been watching us would know that we haven't been home in weeks and it wouldn't take a genius to figure out where we're hiding."

Reed gave a small grin. "If Lamberi thinks you have a good enough reason, he'll believe it. And a good reason will make him think you've even given your security teams the flick."

"And what reason would be good enough for us to do that?" Rachel asked.

Reed hesitated, biting his lip. He shifted, as if sitting back a little—distancing himself. "A reason like the email we deleted from IFRT's relations account this morning before you could see it," he said, looking dead into her eyes, which she was sure had doubled in size.

"What?" she asked, her voice scathing.

"We deleted it because we were suspicious of its origin," Reed said quickly, seeming to watch her carefully, like she might launch at him at any moment. If he was thinking that, he wasn't far off the mark.

"You don't get to delete IFRT business," Rachel said with hard eyes. "That has never been the agreement. Abi doesn't see it, and we're not responding to emails—but you don't delete them."

Reed nodded, but an apology didn't come. "An email came from someone who wanted to meet Abi in Santina. We checked where the email came from, and confirmed its source: the uncle of an Adani civilian. What we don't know is if that person was forced to send the email. James made it very clear at the funeral who was handling security in an attempt to stop something like this from happening, but Lamberi is potentially wounded enough to try. This email could be legit, or it could've been coerced. We'll know once we've checked a few things, but it will take time to do that, and we don't have time."

He looked at her seriously. "The email says this person can meet Abi this evening. If she can't meet this evening, the information will be too old and IFRT won't be able to act on a rescue. There's seventy or more being held in a known location, apparently."

Reed paused, searching her eyes. "Tell me, if you received that email, would your first thought have been how to get rid of your security team so you could make it to that meeting?"

Rachel's jaw ground but she refused to look away. "That is my job."

Reed nodded. "And it's our job to stop you from doing that. I get it, I really do. I think what IFRT does is incredible, but when it comes to our mission, it comes second."

"These people have no one else. No one else will risk their lives to rescue them," Rachel said, her voice rising.

Reed nodded. "I get that, but—"

"No, you *don't*," Rachel said harshly. "We know what we're doing—trust me, we know the risks, because Abi wasn't the first leader to be taken—but if we have information and don't act on it, we have to be able to live with that. We can't. We have to try."

He raised a hand. "So here's the dilemma: we can't verify this email was legit. Yes, it came from someone with no links to Lamberi, but the timing is very coincidental. If we use this to our advantage, though, it will give us two chances to outsmart Lamberi."

Rachel put a hand to her forehead, her head was beginning to ache. "I'm not following."

"We're going to send you and Abi to that meeting. It's in an hour, so we don't have much time to prepare. If it's a legit email, you'll get the information and we'll help you facilitate a rescue—that's our gift for the risk you're taking. If Lamberi is behind it, we'll get a chance to choose the location of the meeting and activate our plan to draw him out. If Lamberi isn't there, our next chance will come later at the time and location he's requested for Abi to be handed over. However, he'll be much more in control of that situation. It's better if we can set the terms and put people in place rather than play his game."

"Asher has agreed to this?" Rachel asked, incredulously.

Reed crossed his arms. "No, Asher has not agreed to this, but we're relying on Abi to get him to agree, because this is a good opportunity to end Lamberi. He's hard to find—he's a nightmare that won't end. The sooner we take him down, the sooner Asher can sleep at night without worrying about him coming after Abi. And Lamberi will; we've always thought it inevitable. Abi has always known it too, and whether Asher wants to deal with it or not, at some point he's going to have to. Abi is being fully briefed now, and if she gives the go ahead, we're relying on her to pacify and convince Asher. We're here to do a job and sometimes he won't like that job."

My job is not to please Asher. It is to make sure he stays alive, and that Santina doesn't fall.

Rachel recalled the words she'd overhead in the hallway, and now it all made sense. She didn't think Reed had been speaking—it had likely been James—but Reed was definitely the person being spoken to.

"If Abi's in, I'm in," Rachel said, and she already knew Abi would go because she'd never be able to live with herself if she played it safe saving her life from Lamberi, but let others—seventy others—be subjected to that fate. Rachel needed to put Daniel on standby.

Reed nodded, and there was something in his eyes, but Rachel still couldn't read him. "I'll give it to you, the two of you are fucking brave."

Rachel felt her cheeks heat up. "Thank you," she said, sounding awkward even to her own ears.

He passed her a phone. "Put your team on standby for the rescue," he said, catching her off guard. He gave a small smile but it transformed his face. "I don't need to be a genius to work out that would be your move after the meeting."

Rachel grinned. "I'm too predictable," she joked, but there was a slither of truth to it—or, rather, insecurity.

Reed didn't miss it. "Predictable is not a word I'd use to describe you. When Abi was taken, none of the moves you made were predictable—except going to the village, which is where anyone with a brain would've started. I'm not sure if you give yourself enough credit," he said, standing. "I need to check in with Abi, and make sure Asher hasn't murdered James," he said with a crooked grin.

He turned and left without another word. Rachel could only imagine the conversations that were being had between James, Abi, and Asher.

Rachel shook her head, returning her attention to the phone in her hand. She messaged Daniel: *Notify team on standby. Be ready to activate in 3 hours.*

His response came a second later: *Activating now.*

ASHER

Asher's jaw hung open and his eyes blazed. James and Reed stood casually, like they were discussing the weather.

"I did not give approval for this," Asher said sharply.

"You need to let us handle the strategy, Asher. This is what we do," James said. "Trust me, I don't like this situation either, but right now it's the best option we have to take out Lamberi. And frankly, we're wasting time we should be spending on strategizing."

Asher shook his head sharply. "That's right, you should be strategizing some other fucking plan, because this one isn't going ahead!"

Asher didn't care that Rachel had agreed to go, it didn't ease any of the crippling fear he felt. He would not put Abi in a position where she was within a hundred miles of Lamberi. Not. A. Chance.

"No. The answer is no," Asher said, resolute.

Abi, who had been quiet until now, finally spoke. "Can you give us a minute?" she asked James, and Asher's blood boiled, heating his entire body.

Reed and James left without a word.

"No," Asher said the moment the door closed. "I can't do this, Abi. I can't." His voice was strained—carrying the weight of the past few months. "How can you even consider this?" he all but screamed. "You told me Lamberi is the one person you wouldn't survive, and now you're willing to risk being put in front of him like bait."

She pressed her lips together, seeming to take a calming breath. "Don't speak to me like I wished for this," she said calmly, but firmly. "I don't want to do this, but I want to be able to live without fearing he's coming after me. He will never stop, Asher. I know men like him, and over and over again he will try to teach you a lesson for taking me back." She sighed. "This is a good opportunity. Look, I'm no security strategist, but I agree it's worth the risk. This could end it, Asher, and then we can both live without fear of him. And the world will be a better place," she said, a plea. "You know what he does to his captives! If Thomas Security can take him out, hundreds—if not thousands—of women and children will never have to be subjected to him. Of all the things I've ever done, this would have the greatest impact. For Santina, and for our entire region, eliminating him will be the greatest gift we can give this world."

Asher began to pace. He understood all that, but he would not let Abi pay the price if it all went wrong. Not to mention the price he would pay if she was taken—hadn't they suffered enough?

"I know all of this, Abi, but it's still not enough. I can't lose you," he said, his panic rising. "I can't. I've almost been there once before, and I might as well have been in hell. If you want Santina—and our region—to flourish, I need to be able to think straight and I can't, not knowing you're anywhere near Lamberi. Let alone if you were taken again."

They stood at a stalemate. Abi's eyes softened, clearly aware of his pain, but he knew she wasn't going to back down. He wanted to fall on the floor and beg her not to do this, but he knew even that wouldn't help. The things he loved about Abi—including how much she cared for others—he hated in that moment, because it was going to tear her away from him.

She took a step toward him, taking his shaking hands. He didn't know if he was shaking from fear or anger.

She put his hands on her hips and draped her arms around his neck.

Asher raised an eyebrow. "If this is an attempt to pacify me—"

"This is an attempt to make the most of a moment alone before I go and do this," she said softly, but there was no mistaking the resoluteness in her voice.

"Abi, please," he said, a final plea. She brushed her lips over his and he shuddered. "I can't lose you, not again," he whispered.

She placed a sweet tender kiss on his lips. "I'm coming back to you. But I need to do this, or else I'll never be able to live with myself."

"And if you do this and something goes wrong, I'll never be able to live with myself," Asher said.

"This is my decision. You're not forcing me—or even encouraging me—so you will be able to live with yourself. I trust this team, and I agree it's better to take on Lamberi on our terms. I can't live the rest of my life in fear of him taking me again, Asher. I can't."

He sighed heavily, resting his forehead against hers, inhaling the sweet, floral scent of her perfume. He prayed like he'd never prayed before that this wasn't the last time he'd hold her.

"Come back to me," he said, feeling like he couldn't breathe.

She looked up at him. "I used to think we weren't meant to be. And now I think we are destined to be, because despite all the odds, and everything that has happened, here we are. Our story isn't over, Asher."

"God I hope you're right," he said, drawing her in, tightening his hold on her. He didn't know how he was going to be able to let go.

He tilted her chin up and his lips found hers. Hungry, savoring, desperate. She deepened the kiss and he kissed her harder. A moan slipped from her lips and it had never sounded sweeter.

He threaded his fingers through her hair, treasuring every second they had together. If life had taught him one thing, it was to never take a moment for granted.

Abi pulled back. "This is the right thing to do," she said with gentle eyes.

Asher shook his head. "I'll never agree with that," he said. Risking her life to save others would never be justifiable for him. He knew that was selfish, but he'd raise hell to protect her.

"But you're not going to stop me," she said, a statement rather than a question, he thought.

How was he supposed to stop her? If he forbade her going, the guilt she would live with for Lamberi's captives, and the fear of always looking over her shoulder, would eat away at them. It would destroy someone like Abi, and eventually she'd end up hating him for it.

But if he let her go, he was going to hate himself if anything went bad.

A knock at the door interrupted them.

"In a minute!" Asher called out, not hiding his annoyance.

He sighed, unable to shake the fear that this would be his last moment alone with Abi.

She looked up through her lashes, searching his eyes.

His lips swept over hers. "I love you, Abi," he said, and she inhaled sharply.

She kissed him. "I love you too," she whispered and his heart swelled.

A second knock at the door signaled James's impatience.

"What?" Asher yelled, noting Abi's somewhat amused expression.

"He knows no boundaries," she whispered under her breath.

"He's a pain in the ass," Asher said, whatever fondness he'd had for James Thomas was rapidly deteriorating.

Abi grinned. "You'll like him again when this is all over," she said as the door swung open and James entered.

Asher didn't agree.

"Lamberi has made contact," James said, looking directly at Asher.

Asher sighed, looking away. He didn't want to face this, and he didn't want to let Abi go, but he knew he was going to have to.

"Let's make a plan," she said, her voice strong and confident.

"It's best if we do this in your office," James said with a nod.

Asher nodded, keeping Abi's hand firm in his. He wasn't ready to let her go, and he wouldn't be anytime soon.

When Asher entered his office, he wasn't surprised to see Reed waiting. A conversation was being had between Reed and Samuel, but it ceased upon Asher's arrival.

"Hi, Asher," Samuel said, almost apologetically. At least someone felt bad for the situation he was in, Asher thought bitterly.

"What are Lamberi's demands?" Asher asked, getting straight to it. He was not in the mood for polite conversation.

James spoke next. "It's worse than we thought," he said, and for the first time Asher thought James actually looked worried.

"How much worse can it get?" Asher said, almost rhetorically.

An image flashed on the screen. A series of green lines formed, overlaying the map of Santina. "What is that?" Asher asked.

James paused for a moment. "It's Santina's water supply," he said, grim.

Asher felt like James had punched him in the stomach. "No," he said, his voice hoarse. "What about the bombers?"

"They're only one part of this. The second part is the water supply. If you don't hand over Abi, he's going to contaminate all of Santina's water. You can't—"

"I'm very aware I can't let that happen," Asher said sharply. "Tell me how he can do that. Shouldn't we have security in place to prevent things like this happening?"

"You should, yes, but someone is helping him. Someone who has something to gain from Santina falling—someone who knows Santina's operations well," James said. "I think that person is Martin Snider."

"Did he help Lamberi enter Santina too?" Asher asked.

James sighed. "We don't know yet, but I'd bet my life on it," he said, and he didn't sound happy. It pleased Asher to see some kind of emotional response from him, but he wanted him to be angry—he wanted him to be as furious as Asher was.

"Right now, the focus is on drawing Lamberi out. When we do, he's going to find himself in a world of pain that he could never have imagined," James said. There was a slight purr to his voice, but not that of a house cat—it sounded more like a lion waking up. Asher didn't know whether to be comforted by the fact that a guy so chillingly cold was protecting him, or to install another lock on his door.

"We need to find Martin Snider," Asher said. He was sick of

hearing that name, but knowing little else about him, he wondered again if it was a coincidence that the alias this person had chosen had the same given name as his father.

"I think Lamberi is probably the only one who has seen him. Martin Snider has never shown his face to anyone, but Lamberi isn't a fool, and he's not going to do business with someone he's never met. Lamberi will know who Martin Snider is, and then we'll find him," James said. Asher searched his eyes, only to find that they were dark wells of confidence.

"I need you to go now," James said. "It'll be easier for you if you don't know the plan."

Asher's jaw fell open. "What? No."

"Please let us handle this, Asher."

"I am letting you handle it, but if you think I'm letting Abi do this without consulting on the plan, then you're out of your mind! And I'm staying connected while she's out there. I'm not on board, and the only reason this damn plan is happening is because I can't convince Abi not to do it," Asher said, crossing his arms over his chest.

Through the screen, Asher saw Samuel's eyes darting to James. He looked concerned, and he should be, because Asher wasn't backing down. He didn't care how they did things, he needed to be involved regardless of whether he was of any help or not.

"Okay," James said, not sounding even a little thrilled about it. "You'll stay here with Jesse and Samuel, and you'll be connected throughout. But I'm telling you now, you don't give anyone an order throughout this mission. I have men on the ground, Abi and Rachel are on the ground, and I need my men to think straight and not worry about orders coming through from the king. They don't need a single distraction. I'm asking them to risk their lives, and they take that risk because they trust me. I won't have my men dying because orders are confused." There was a fire in James's eyes, but he had nothing to worry about—Asher had no intention of giving any orders, but he sure as hell wasn't going to sit in his living quarters while this was going on.

"You have my word," Asher said.

James nodded then turned to Samuel. "Connect Asher's office in so that he has full access to the footage."

Samuel nodded.

Asher's door opened and Reed and Rachel entered. Rachel was chewing on her cheek, and she looked nervous. Asher didn't blame her.

Rachel's eyes landed on Abi and she looked resigned, like they were two women with bombs strapped to their chests.

"Okay," James said, "vests." He passed them a bulletproof vest each. "Put this on now, because I want you to get used to the weight. If Lamberi—or any of his men watching—notice something is amiss, they won't hesitate to act."

Rachel and Abi left the office to put their vests on and Asher returned his attention to Samuel.

"Have we responded, confirming the meeting?" Asher asked.

Samuel nodded. "Yes, and the reply has been received. We went in and prepped the location we chose, and then sent the email giving the building address. If anyone was watching the building after that email was sent, they'll see nothing, because our men are already in place and are so hidden that even if Lamberi's men search the building they'll never find them."

"Where are they hiding?" Asher asked, trying to distract himself.

"In some concealed cavities in the tunnels below the restaurant. I found them on some old blueprints from the Santina council department," he said, seemingly pleased with himself.

Asher opened his mouth to inquire further but Abi returned with Rachel. He watched her walk. "How is your back?" he asked.

"It's fine," she said.

He hated that word. Fine never meant good; fine was the mediocrity of all things.

"It's hurting you," Asher said, but she shook her head defiantly.

"It's okay, and it'll hurt much less than a bullet," she said.

James nodded in apparent approval. "It's just for a few hours and then we'll take it off you. Take these," he said, extending his hand to reveal two white pills. "It'll help with the pain and any ache that sets in, but the dose is low enough that it won't have any side effects."

Asher wondered if James should've asked when she ate last before giving her the medication, but he probably already knew.

Abi popped the pills out of the plastic and swallowed two.

"So this is the plan," James said. "We're leaving in twenty minutes. We're going to drop Abi and Rachel here." He pointed at a map that flashed on the screen. "It'll take you about fifteen minutes to walk to the location. That's longer than I would like, but we're concerned that if we drop you any closer, Lamberi's men might see. So, it's actually safer if you walk the distance. You'll wear a baseball hat and sunglasses until you reach the building—that's both for Lamberi's men and for the public. The last thing we need is Abi attracting attention and getting stopped on the street."

James looked to Abi, but Asher didn't think he was seeking approval. Abi nodded regardless.

"You'll enter through the main door and proceed down to the basement restaurant. Restaurants are common meeting grounds for criminals; we like them because they're crowded, and therefore it's less likely to cause a scene, because there are too many witnesses." James paused, then added, "Less likely, but that doesn't mean it won't happen. If this is a setup and not a legitimate lead, Lamberi will be ready to attack at any time. If I were him, I'd attempt an attack before you even step foot inside the restaurant. That said, there may be other factors involved that we aren't aware of, so we need to be prepared for all situations."

Asher felt like his throat was thickening and maybe he should've left when James had told him to.

"And if it is a legitimate lead, is our informant going to be compromised?" Abi asked, and Asher marveled once again at her ability to think of others when she herself was going through so much.

"We'll protect the informant," James said, not elaborating.

Reed opened a bag and passed Rachel and Abi a hat and pair of sunglasses each.

Invisible chains constricted around Asher's chest, and he felt like he was sending Abi to a certain death—or worse.

He saw James eyeing him carefully, and he put on the best poker face he could manage, but Asher wasn't sure how convincing it was.

"Let's go," James said.

ABI

*J*ames Thomas walked beside her. "How are you feeling?"

"Nervous," Abi replied.

James nodded. "That's not a bad thing. Being alert and cautious will save your life. People die when they get complacent and overconfident." He looked over his shoulder and said, "Confirm."

Abi didn't bother asking—she knew James would only tell her what she needed to know and right now, she didn't think she could handle much more.

She thought she'd prepared herself, but it was only once they were in the car and exiting the palace that the gravity of what she was about to do set in. She blocked the memory of the anguish in Asher's eyes as they'd said goodbye.

"Come back to me," he'd whispered with a choked-up voice.

"If you hadn't escaped in Adani, would you rather have survived and been taken by Lamberi, or would you have wished for death?" James asked her slowly.

She met his eyes, and she realized Asher wasn't the only troubled one. "Death," she answered.

He sighed heavily, seeming to weigh something in his mind.

"Then take this," he said, handing her a single white pill. "I'm going to be close to you the entire time, Abi. I'm going to do everything I can, and I've never lost a client, but," he said, his voice sounding strained, "I understand what being taken by Lamberi means. If everything goes horribly wrong—which it won't," he added quickly. "But as a worst-case scenario, this is a cyanide pill. However, if you find yourself in his hands, give me time to get you back because I will shift heaven and earth to make that happen."

"How long is long enough?" she asked, swallowing hard.

"Ninety-six hours," he said, and she knew why he said that: if captives weren't found after ninety-six hours, they were almost always never seen again.

Abi sucked in a breath and her hand trembled as she reached for the pill. It was so small, so deadly, and she stared at it for a moment. She tucked the pill into her jeans pocket, making a mental note to destroy it when this was over and done with.

"You didn't tell Asher about this, did you?" Abi asked.

"No," he said, unapologetically. "It'll only cause him to worry about things he can't control. I've been where he is right now, and it's a horrible position to be in."

Abi paused, taken aback by his honesty.

"You let your girlfriend walk into the enemy's hands?" Abi asked incredulously.

James chewed on his cheek. "Yes, but that's a long story. The enemy was actually her missing husband—he's dead now, and she's safe. She's my wife now, by the way," he said, seeming proud of himself.

Abi was at a loss for words. She was surprised he'd freely given that information to her—maybe he'd done it to calm her and distract her—and if that was so, it had worked because now all she could think of was the missing husband and who he'd been.

"You wouldn't believe it even if I told you," he said, correctly guessing where her mind had gone. "And I'm not going to tell you."

"Let's make a deal," Abi said. James raised his eyebrows but nodded, indicating he would hear her out at least. "If I survive this, you tell me that story," she said.

James grinned and she was surprised he could smile at a moment like this. But then again, she knew it wasn't his first rodeo. "Deal, Abigail Bennett," James said.

They were silent for the rest of the trip but Abi's mind was busy crafting scenarios of how James's wife had faced off her missing husband. Had James killed him? Was it weird if he had?

"Game time," James said as the car came to a stop. Abi looked out the window, shocked they'd arrived so quickly. His method of distracting her had worked and she was surprised to find she felt measurably calmer than she had when they'd left the palace. She even noted James's choice of words. *Game time*—maybe that was how he coped with the many stressful situations he found himself in. Perhaps he looked at it like a challenge, or a game. Abi opted to take that approach now, because the reality was far too frightening.

She looked over her shoulder to see a second car pull up behind her. How was Rachel right now? She was risking her life, and possibly ending up in Lamberi's hands, for Abi.

Abi exhaled a shaky breath.

James passed her another weapon. "Just in case, but I have your back."

All words of thanks lodged in her throat. She stared at the weapon for a moment—it was all too real.

"Game time," James repeated with a little more conviction.

"Game time," Abi said as she saw Rachel approach the car. "Game time," she whispered again, this time under her breath.

She took one last look at James Thomas, hoping like hell he knew what he was doing and that he was every bit as good as she needed him to be.

Abi tucked the additional weapon into the holster underneath her sweater. The walk to the meeting point was going to make her ankle ache, but they didn't have any other option. She agreed James could hardly drop her off at the front entrance.

She looked at Rachel and tried to give her a look of confidence. Rachel managed a small smile, but Abi knew there was nothing behind it. This was more than they'd trained for. More than they had ever experienced.

"We're going to be okay," Abi said, to herself as much as to Rachel.

Rachel smiled tightly. "Of course we are."

"Do you know that James's wife faced off her missing husband and James killed him? She was his girlfriend then, and is his wife now," Abi said, trying to distract Rachel.

"Huh," she said as they walked. "He told you that?"

"That's what you call a tease, right?" Abi asked, watching the streets carefully. She knew James had teams planted at every point along the street, but she would need to be alert too, if she was going to survive.

"He doesn't seem like the talkative type," Rachel said, looking over her shoulder.

"Look straight ahead," Abi whispered. "I think he was trying to distract me, to calm me down. It worked, and I can't wait to hear the rest of that story."

"I get the feeling that James, and everyone in that company, is full of stories," she said.

"Including Reed," Abi said, stealing a sideways glance. She'd said it to test Rachel, but she was still trying to distract her mind enough that if they encountered trouble she'd be able to think and not freeze up. Rachel had proven herself on the field, but off the field was a different game. They knew the rules on the field when they were conducting IFRT business. Here, in Santina, facing Lamberi—they had no idea what the rules were.

"Yes, Reed," Rachel said like she didn't care, but Abi thought Rachel had wondered about his past on more than a few occasions.

Informant has arrived early. Continue ahead, James said through Abi's earpiece. Abi pressed her earlobe, activating two-way communication.

"Copy," Abi said under her breath.

"Do you think it's weird that the informant came early?" Rachel asked, keeping her gaze straight ahead.

"I don't know," Abi said, but she knew they were going to find out soon.

"*Informant looks nervous,*" James said.

Abi considered that. It wasn't necessarily surprising—supplying IFRT with knowledge could land informants in serious trouble.

"Copy. That's normal," Abi communicated, covering her mouth like she was coughing.

"*Informant has been seated at our table of choice,*" James informed.

Abi exhaled—everything was going according to plan. She prayed that continued.

Abi's phone beeped and she opened her messages as she walked. There was one from James Thomas and it was a picture of a woman.

Abi frowned. The woman seemed familiar, but Abi couldn't place her.

"Who is this?" Abi asked.

"*Your informant,*" James said.

Abi almost tripped on her feet. "She's female. It's rare that we meet female informants. Females usually keep quiet because they will pay a greater price if they're discovered to have given information." Abi was looking at Rachel, as if she was speaking to her, but something—or rather, someone—caught her attention.

Troy.

He looked up, his eyes narrowing at something ahead. Abi followed his gaze, but she saw nothing unusual.

"James, Asher's cousin Troy is here," she said under her breath. "We're walking past him now."

"*We see him,*" James said. "*Keep going, he hasn't recognized you. We'll keep an eye on him.*"

"Is he a suspect?" Abi asked, fighting to keep her face neutral. Abi thought Troy was one of the only few people Asher had left that he trusted.

"*Everyone is a suspect until confirmed otherwise,*" James said but there was no tone to his voice. He said it like he could be talking about her own mother. "*Keep walking, you're right on time.*"

Abi had refrained from looking at her wrist in case someone was watching, and she was relieved to hear they were on time. If this was a legitimate lead, the informant wouldn't wait around for them—not to mention that her ankle was beginning to throb and the sooner she was there and could sit down for a minute the better.

"Troy's not following you," James said.

Abi supposed that should've given her some relief, but it was strange he had been there in the first place.

"He lives in an apartment only a few blocks from here," James said, once again accurately guessing where her mind had gone.

"Copy," Abi said as their location came into view.

"We have your back and we have men inside," James said. "Follow my lead and don't make a move until I tell you to." It was more of a warning than an instruction, and Abi remembered the warning Asher had been given in his office.

Abi's pulse quickened, and she wished she could give Rachel a hug or squeeze her hand. But it was too late for that. Now they had to muster all their courage as they walked into the lion's den.

Abi drew in a long, settling breath as she climbed the few short steps into the restaurant. She refrained from looking directly at the informant—which took all the willpower she had—but she did a quick scope of the restaurant, which she would've done on official IFRT business. If anyone was watching her, that wasn't out of the ordinary. Then her eyes landed on the informant and Abi was sure she'd seen her somewhere before. If she had, that could be a good thing, as she might've seen her during a village visit. Abi would know when the informant told her which village she belonged to.

And then Abi really wanted to know how the woman had gotten into Santina.

The hostess led Abi and Rachel to the table and they took a seat. The informant had trouble meeting their eyes, and that either meant something was wrong, or she'd been a captive herself. If so, she definitely wasn't a captive IFRT had rescued—the faces of those women were imprinted in Abi's mind.

"Hello," Abi said gently. "Thank you for meeting us. We know the risks of taking such a step and we promise that whatever information you give us, we will make sure we use it to help people. This meeting won't be for nothing."

The woman cleared her throat. "Many captives . . . too many . . ." She looked around nervously. "Location on map," she said, visibly swallowing.

She reached for her bag.

"*Hold,*" James's warning came through her earpiece. "*I have a weapon on her. Don't move.*"

Abi didn't get up, but she placed her hand on her lap, ready to reach for her weapon if she needed. She doubted she could move that quickly if the woman suddenly pointed a gun at her, but damn if she wouldn't try.

But the woman pulled out a piece of folded paper and slid it across the table. She'd hesitated a fraction of a second and Abi's own hand trembled as she reached for the paper.

She unfolded it and her heart lurched as she did. It was a map of Adani, but it was the hastily scribbled writing that made her brain scream the written words.

RUN.

ABI

*R*UN.

"*Don't move!*" James said.

Every instinct told her to move, and the restaurant seemed to stop, like it was frozen in time. It even seemed silent, and Abi knew there was no way that could be true. But in that moment her world stopped.

Lamberi was here and she knew it.

"*Do* not *move!*" James yelled more urgently.

Abi wanted to run, but she felt like James had somehow injected her legs with something and they were like dead logs attached to her body.

"I'm sorry," the informant whispered. "He's going to kill my family."

"Who?" Abi asked, surprised she managed to force the words from her throat.

"Martin. He walked past you as you walked in," the woman said, her words rushed.

Abi's breath hitched in her throat. Surely James had footage of that. "Where is he now?" Abi asked, glad her mind was working even if her legs weren't.

"*No one walked past you, Abi. She's lying,*" James said.

Abi's fear transformed to anger. What game was this woman playing? Why had she told Abi to run? To create chaos so she'd potentially lose any security guards that had followed her?

"I don't know," she said, shaking her head.

"Do you have a daughter?" Abi asked, knowing James wasn't going to like her next words.

"Yes," the woman answered, but Abi didn't know if it was a lie or not.

"Then you'd better pray she never meets someone like me," Abi said.

The woman went still. "Why?" she asked, but Abi never got the chance to answer.

Thunder boomed and cracked and Abi reached for Rachel as they dove to the floor. People began screaming and James was saying something through her earpiece, but she couldn't hear him. Abi looked up to see the legs of the informant still sitting in her chair. Abi's stomach churned when she realized the woman wasn't moving at all—an odd thing given the restaurant had erupted into chaos. People were running now, and they were all headed for the back of the restaurant.

They had to move.

"Come on!" Abi said, tugging Rachel's hand.

Abi peered up while staying as low as she could underneath the table. She saw men fighting at the front and bodies lying all over the ground. Some were missing limbs and she knew they'd been killed by the explosion and thrown across the restaurant.

Abi refrained from gagging as she realized a severed, charcoaled arm had landed not far from her.

"*Back! Go to the back!*" James said, her earpiece clear once again.

Rachel must've heard it too, because she was on her feet and running with Abi.

Abi focused ahead, but she couldn't forget the last thing she'd seen before they'd run from the table—their *informant* with a bullet between her eyes.

Someone pushed Abi in the back and she hissed in a breath.

Between her back and her ankle she was hardly in shape to run, but she knew she'd be dead if she stayed.

Rachel's grip on Abi's arm tightened, keeping her upright. It wasn't lost on Abi that Rachel was once again by her side when she needed her most.

A figure came sprinting from the side and Abi's first reaction was to draw her weapon. She realized in the last moment it was Reed, and her finger slackened on the trigger. "Easy," he said calmly as he guided them toward the restaurant kitchen.

People were running in all directions and the gunfire was deafening. Abi didn't stop to look over her shoulder. How many were shooting? How many were Thomas Security's men? How many were Lamberi's?

Abi decided it didn't matter.

She needed to focus on themselves and with Rachel and now Reed by her side, their chances had just greatly increased.

"Go! Go! Go!" Reed said as he flung open a door. Rachel didn't hesitate as she ran into the darkness. Abi followed, and it took more than a few minutes for her eyes to adjust. James had said they'd chosen this location for a reason—for the exit possibilities—but Abi hadn't fully realized the extent of the exit possibilities.

The back of the kitchen had led into a maze of tunnels not unlike those underneath the palace, but Abi quickly realized she didn't like tunnels without Asher. She felt claustrophobic and she hated the darkness that seemed to seep into her lungs, making it hard to breathe. Or perhaps it was fear that was suffocating her; Abi didn't know.

"Let's go!" Reed said, grabbing Rachel's hand. Rachel had Abi's hand and they ran ahead. Reed had a small flashlight—he had obviously been prepared for this—but the light it provided was minimal. Abi didn't think that was an accident, as it was just enough power to light their path but not enough to light up the tunnel and potentially alert their enemies they were coming until it was too late for them to react.

Abi's ankle was throbbing and it felt like it had doubled in size, but she didn't stop to check. She blocked out the pain because she knew the pain of being taken by Lamberi would be much greater. She thought of the white pill in her pocket, and what she and James hadn't spoken about. If she didn't take the pill before ninety-six hours, she'd likely never have the chance. And if she took it too early, he might come for her and find she'd already killed herself.

As they ran through the dark tunnel, Abi decided she wouldn't take that pill. But if the opportunity came, she would hide it, and remember exactly where she placed it. If she was still there a few weeks later, she'd take it if she could get to it.

Abi heard footsteps in the tunnel and they were moving fast. In the darkness she felt disoriented, and she wasn't sure if the footsteps were ahead of or behind them. She didn't know who they belonged to, but given that Reed's pace had quickened, she assumed they didn't belong to Thomas Security.

Abi stumbled, unable to keep up any longer. Despite her best attempts to block out the pain, she couldn't. "Go! Get out of here!" she said to Rachel.

Reed came to a halt and pushed them up against the wall of the tunnel. He turned and fired as two figures emerged behind them. The bodies fell, but not before they fired back.

Abi would've sighed in relief, but she could hear more footsteps, and it didn't sound like one or two people.

It sounded like an army.

JAMES

"Samuel, they're not here!" James exclaimed as he came to a stop.

His shoulder was bleeding from a knife wound and he'd narrowly avoided a bullet to the back of his head. One of his guys had pushed him aside a second before the trigger had been pulled.

He pulled out his phone again, checking the GPS.

"Fuck," he swore under his breath. It had been a while since he'd been in a situation that had escalated so fast. In a matter of seconds, everything had shifted and their entire plan had blown up along with the front of the building. It had been a smart move by their enemies because it had created pandemonium and forced everyone to the back of the restaurant. It had also blocked more of James's men from entering.

"*They should be there!*" Samuel insisted.

James turned in a circle, pivoting on his feet. His weapon raised, his finger on the trigger.

"The GPS is off, maybe it's the tunnels. They're not here," James said, knowing he'd have to do this blind—without Samuel's help.

"*Let me try and amplify Reed's tracker. Give me a second,*" Samuel said, but as James heard stomping footsteps—those that could only belong to running men—he knew he didn't have a second. James pressed his back flush against the tunnel wall. He held steady, poised. He knew from the sound of the footsteps they weren't his men. His men didn't run heavy like that, they were quieter—they'd been trained to run like ghosts. Men who ran with these heavy footsteps were soldiers, men who had been trained on battlefields.

Three, two, one.

James fired, taking down men as they ran around the curve of the tunnel. One by one they fell, but there were too many of them, and they fired back. Luckily for James, their aim was off—these guys weren't used to shooting on the run—and James pulled a grenade from his back pocket and launched it. He ran backward, shielding his head with his arms as the explosion lit up the tunnel. He paused for a few seconds and then looked up. No one emerged from the blast. No one moved.

"James. I can't be sure, but if the signal is correct, Reed is farther down the tunnel. It doesn't look like he's moving."

James didn't like the sound of that and his stomach churned. They should be running—they should be out of the tunnels by now.

"Copy," James said, sprinting forward.

He kept his flashlight aimed at the ground and used the tunnel wall to guide him. He felt like he was running into a black abyss.

"Reed!" James shouted.

Reed responded, but his voice came through as a series of fragmented sentences broken up by static. James couldn't make out a word he was saying. They'd tested the earpieces in the tunnel earlier and they'd worked, and the GPS signals had worked too. If James had known they were going to have these issues he'd never have chosen this location. Tunnels were great until you were trapped in one end of them with no way out. He could only assume the breakdown of communication had something to do with the explosion at the front of the building.

More static followed. *"Abi . . . Rachel . . ."* were the only two words James could make out.

He pushed his legs harder, sprinting forward. As long as he was heading in the right direction, and they were still in the tunnel, he'd have to run into them sooner or later.

James hurdled almost a second too late, and just clipped the edge of the fallen body. He stumbled, barely catching himself. He swung around, weapon raised. He pointed his flashlight on the two bodies heaped against the tunnel wall. Bullets to the chest.

A flicker of hope burned in his chest.

These weren't his men, and chances were Reed had taken them out.

His new recruit was deadly—with his hands and his weapon—which was the only reason James had entrusted him with this mission. Normally, he'd never promote a new recruit so fast, but there was something about Reed that frightened even James a little. He had supernatural instincts, and he moved faster than anyone James had ever seen—and he'd trained and assessed a lot of men in his time.

Lethal: that was the one word James used to describe him.

"... Lamberi ..." James's heart skipped a beat. He missed the full sentence, but there was no mistaking that name.

James surged ahead, his heart pounding in his chest.

He would not let Lamberi take Abi.

He would not allow it.

ABI

Abi recognized him before she heard Reed say his name.

Their eyes met, and even in the darkness of the tunnel, Abi saw a gleam of arrogance in them. Lamberi thought he had them cornered, and he might be right, but Abi was not going without a fight.

Abi grabbed Rachel and stepped in front of her, shielding her—but as she did, she had taken her eyes off Lamberi for a moment, and in that single moment, a team of men had appeared around him, protecting him.

A cunning grin spread across his lips, but it faltered when Abi drew her weapon and started firing. She didn't think about it, and she didn't hesitate. Those years of training were paying off. And when you're facing death—or worse—courage has a way of finding its way to the surface.

She heard an awful crack behind her—the sound of something breaking, likely someone's neck. The distraction caused her to lose focus for a second, and bullets started chipping the ground around her.

"Rachel!" Abi screamed, reaching for her, making sure she was still shielded, because even amid the chaos Abi knew one thing—Lamberi wanted her alive.

She heard Reed hiss, like he'd been shot. Determination rose like an overflowing dam in a storm, but her breath stuck in her throat when she realized her weapon was empty. She reached for the second pistol James had given her but it was gone. She must've dropped it. The walls of the tunnel seemed to shift and the blood in her veins went cold.

No!

She was not giving in.

Rachel screamed behind her and her hand was ripped from Abi's. Abi spun around, her need to protect her friend stronger than any other thought in her mind.

But Reed lunged through the air and delivered a blow to the temple of the man dragging Rachel. He fell to the ground but Reed delivered a second blow—making sure he didn't get up. Abi wondered why Reed didn't just shoot him, and then a sickening realization settled in.

Reed was out of ammunition too.

Abi swung around as Lamberi's men lunged for her. She had her pistol in her hand. It didn't have any bullets, but her arm flung, mirroring Reed's a moment ago and hit the temple of the man closest to her. He fell, but another was right behind him, pointing a pistol at Abi's forehead.

"Lower your weapons," Lamberi growled.

Abi couldn't move. She was frozen in place.

"Lower your weapons," he repeated, less patient.

Slowly, her arm lowered—and then she realized he'd said *weapons*.

Abi didn't need to look behind her to realize he was talking to Reed as well.

Her heart stammered violently against her ribs.

"Run," Abi whispered to Rachel. "Run!" she urged in a hushed whisper.

But Rachel didn't move. Instead, Abi felt something slide into her back pocket. Something hard, something metal.

Abi met the gaze of the man pointing his pistol to her head.

She would play his game—for now. Besides, she thought darkly, she couldn't reach the other weapon if she didn't lower the empty one in her hand.

She heard movement behind her and knew Reed had lowered his weapon and put it on the ground. She prayed Rachel had passed him a second weapon.

"Get out of here," Abi whispered again when she didn't hear Rachel move.

"Can't," she said, and it was only then Abi realized there must be men behind them too. They were cornered in the tunnel.

Where was James Thomas?

The silence in the tunnel was deafening and unease clung to her skin like cobwebs.

"You should never have run from me, Abigail," Lamberi said, drawing her attention back to him. The sound of his voice gave her chills—it was as cold as his soul. The corner of his lips turned up. "I do like a fighter, though."

Abi's stomach churned violently. "You chose the wrong fighter to come after." She all but spat the words at him.

He raised an eyebrow. "You did this to yourself the night you killed my brother."

Abi blinked, her mind refusing to communicate with her mouth. No quick reply came. Nothing came at all.

His brother? She didn't even know he'd had a brother.

The night on the side of the highway to Santina, Abi realized.

She felt cold to her bones. Maybe the colonel hadn't been killed because he was close to Asher—maybe he'd been killed because he'd helped Abi.

She wanted to be sick, but somehow she managed to keep it together.

"I didn't kill your brother," Abi said shakily.

"You did. I saw you do it," he said, his voice menacing.

He took a step forward. Abi didn't move; she couldn't. How could he have seen her? He wasn't there.

A cunning smile spread across his lips and he looked terrifying. There was something abnormal in his eyes. He didn't look human in that moment. He looked possessed.

"Don't worry. I'm going to tell—"

His voice was drowned out by an explosion behind him, and then the gunfire that followed was so deafening every bang seemed to echo in Abi's head. She could barely see straight, let alone think straight.

And Lamberi used that to his advantage.

He lunged for her, and she didn't move fast enough.

He grabbed her arms and pulled her into his arms. Her back was flush against his chest and she was cold with fear.

"You're my queen now, beautiful," he said, his lips on her neck.

Abi looked to Reed, who was fighting off the group of men behind him. His eyes kept darting to her, never losing sight of her. But he couldn't fight ten men and rescue her at the same time. Lamberi's hand pressed flat against her stomach, just above her pelvic bone and his touch made her reel.

She was not going without a fight.

Never.

She drew a deep breath, which seemed impossible to do while in Lamberi's arms. He turned, ready to drag her away, and that's when she saw the war going on behind her.

There were bodies lining the ground and Lamberi's men were using them as shields. There was an invisible line in the tunnel, and then she saw the Thomas Security men—dressed in full SWAT gear—moving fast and without pause. Abi couldn't make out any strategy but they must've had one because there were far fewer of their men on the ground.

Lamberi was inching backward, and Abi couldn't see where Reed was. Was he still alive?

Abi steeled herself, knowing she'd only have one chance.

One chance to kill Lamberi.

She pushed everything from her mind: the gunfire, the fear, the sick feeling swirling in her stomach.

She focused on her anger—and only that.

It lit a fire inside her and then she moved fast. Lamberi's grip had loosened a little, not much, but enough to catch him by surprise.

She jolted her arms, slamming her elbow into his stomach as her heel came up, slamming between his legs. It wasn't enough to knock him to the floor, but his grip loosened again.

She sprinted forward, needing to put enough distance between them that she could pull her pistol and shoot.

But Lamberi wasn't giving up. His hands caught the edge of her shirt and he reeled her back in.

Abi delivered an elbow to his chin and he lost his grip once again. She couldn't think straight—all she could think to do was run. Her legs burned as she ran past Reed. She didn't see Rachel among the chaos but if Lamberi was chasing her, he couldn't take Rachel.

She heard footsteps behind her and knew they were Lamberi's. She didn't know how close he was, but she felt like he was going to reach out and grab her at any second.

She saw an intersection in the tunnel and turned sharply. Lamberi skidded behind her, but his footsteps continued to hunt hers. She hadn't thought this through, she realized, because this tunnel was like a black hole and she couldn't see a thing. All she could sense was his breathing behind her.

More footsteps seemed to be following, but she thought the darkness was playing tricks on her mind. A tiny light on the tunnel wall indicated another turn and she took it, then found herself immediately hating the decision. She was running farther into the maze with no idea how to get out.

Her T-shirt tightened as she was pulled backward, and she knew it was over.

"No!" she screamed as his hand wrapped around her waist, drawing her in. He slammed her against the tunnel wall and the back of her head bounced against the rock.

"I'm going to have so much fun with you," he whispered, his lips on her neck. She gagged, and it only seemed to please him. He pressed his body flat against hers, pinning her to the tunnel wall. Abi didn't know if he was getting off on it, or using the maneuver simply as a method to restrain her.

"Queen Abigail," he said, breathless. "It has a nice ring to it. I can't wait to see Asher's face when I send him photos of us."

Acrid bile rose in her throat and, as he pressed his hips against hers, the gun in her back pocket dug into her hip.

"Please don't do this," she said, changing the tone of her voice. He liked a fighter, and every time she fought, it only seemed to encourage him.

He laughed against her neck. "That won't work on me, sweetie," he said, his lips moving up her soft skin. His face was in the curve of her neck and she mustered every ounce of energy she had to raise her knee into his groin and slam her shoulder into his face. Unprepared, he faltered, recoiling in pain.

She twisted as she reached for her back pocket.

Lamberi pulled her back in with a snarl, but he was a second too late.

Her pistol was aimed at his stomach and she pulled the trigger.

Blood sprayed over her chest and she froze. Her mind wasn't working properly, but she knew there was too much blood.

Lamberi gurgled and swayed on his feet. "You bitch!" he growled.

Abi fired again, terrified he was going to somehow recover. In the faint flow of the small lights on the tunnel wall, he didn't look human. He looked like a monster—like the devil.

When he fell to his knees, an arm reached around, pulling her back. She screamed and fought, thrashing wildly.

"It's me, it's James! I've got you," he said and she surrendered, her legs giving way. James caught her, dragging her backward.

James spoke again, his voice now impossibly calm. "You're okay," he whispered again.

"I'm bleeding," she whispered, noting her wet shirt. She couldn't feel any pain, and that worried her more than anything.

"What?" James asked, his calm voice replaced by a frantic, higher note. He grabbed his light, running it over her. "Where does it hurt?"

Abi shook her head, beginning to feel lightheaded. "The blood, it's everywhere."

"It's not your blood, Abi," he said quickly.

Her vision blurred and the walls of darkness seemed to shift. She didn't know if she was having a panic attack or bleeding to death.

"Look at me! Look at me!" James said. "It's not your blood."

A figure came hurdling over the bodies and James swung around, raising the weapon he'd taken from Abi's hand.

He faltered, and Abi realized he'd seen him the moment she had.

"I'm out of ammunition," Reed said quickly, and James threw him two pistols.

"Let's go!" James said, keeping hold of Abi's arm.

"Where's Rachel?" Abi asked in a panic. Why wasn't she with Reed?

"She's out of the tunnels; she's safe," he said, and Abi breathed a sigh of relief. "I had a little trouble finding you," he continued, and it sounded like an apology.

James had Abi's arm and they ran. She was through the next corner of the tunnel when she realized her ankle wasn't aching. She could barely feel anything. She felt like she was floating. She remembered the blood, which no one except her seemed that worried about.

"Move to exit six," James commanded beside her as they ran.

She had no idea what he was talking about but he didn't seem to be talking to her anyway.

They ran for what seemed like forever. Slowly the tunnel grew quiet and the only sounds were their footsteps.

"Slow down," James commanded, and Abi sighed with relief. Reed seemed to be completely unaffected by the run.

They slowed to a walk, but James ran ahead. He opened a door that Abi was sure she would've missed if she'd been alone. Men filtered out and by the organization and lack of gunfire she knew they were Thomas Security men.

They encircled Abi and helped her through the door and into the daylight. The sun had begun to set, but after being in the pitch-dark tunnels, it was like staring into a spotlight. Abi squinted, casting her eyes down. She'd lost all sense of time completely. It had seemed like the middle of the night in the tunnel and she wondered how long they'd been in there.

They were ushered into cars and it was only once they were moving that James looked over her. His gaze dropped to her chest and she was scared to look.

"It's Lamberi's blood," he said.

"I shot him in the stomach," Abi said, shaking her head.

James grinned in appreciation. "And I shot him from behind, which caused this mess."

Abi paused, finally looking down. She felt her chest and abdomen, and it wasn't her blood. She wasn't bleeding, just like James had said. She wondered if James shooting Lamberi from behind had been a risky move when the bullet could've gone through him and hit her, and then she remembered she was wearing a vest.

She exhaled a shaky breath of relief.

"Sorry I couldn't give you any warning. I don't know what happened to our ear pieces," James said, his lips forming a thin line. "We tested them in the tunnels earlier, but something caused interference." James met her gaze. "You're a brave woman, Abi. You did well today."

Abi didn't feel brave at all. She felt like she'd been fighting to keep her herself together throughout the entire ordeal.

James looked to Rachel. "The same to you, Rachel. Normally, I would never send two clients in like we did with you both because they wouldn't cope. I've only ever done it on a few occasions, and they were exceptions—not because of the mission, but because of *who* was being sent in. You both handled it better than I thought you were going to. We're used to this, and we've been trained for it. I know you do some training with IFRT, but training is never as good as field experience. With new recruits, they start on very small jobs, getting a feel for being in the field and managing the adrenaline. They slowly work their way up once I know they can think under pressure." He paused, grinning. "You did better than any of my new recruits would've done. Don't tell Asher I said this, but if you ever want a job, give me a call," he told them, and Abi could tell he was only half-kidding.

Abi mustered a smile, because what else was there to do?

James turned serious. "Lamberi is dead. I double-checked before we left, and I took some DNA to see if we can get a match to any medical records." He shrugged. "We might not get that lucky. But the bullet in his stomach killed him, and the one in his shoulder added to his pain. There's no doubt about it. Now Asher can focus on Santina without worrying about Lamberi coming after you," James said, looking at Abi.

Abi cleared her throat. "But do you think his men will retaliate for his death?"

James chewed on his cheek. "I don't know, but it's possible."

"Then Asher still has to worry," Abi said with a sigh.

"Asher is always going to have to worry about something," James said. "That's part of his title. But I can promise you there's a difference between those worries, and someone specifically coming for someone you love. That's a different level of torture completely. There's nothing worse," he said, his voice sounding far away.

"That reminds me . . ." Abi started wryly. "You owe me a story."

ASHER

He paced the hallway, his mind a murky pond of thoughts. He was relieved and he was angry—he didn't know whether to kill James Thomas or thank him. Lamberi was dead, and that gave him a sense of peace that nothing else could've, but it crippled him to think about the price Abi had almost paid.

"You're going to wear a hole in the floor," Jesse said gently.

Asher sighed. He'd been surprised when James had said Jesse would stay behind with the teams and provide security for Asher. From the last conversations he'd had with Thomas Security, Jesse still hadn't been cleared.

Asher had felt a soothing sense of relief when James had told him Jesse would stay. He hadn't realized how much questioning Jesse had impacted him.

Jesse had been with his family since Asher was born. He'd been loyal to King Martin—as far as Asher knew—and they'd never had a reason not to trust him. But more than that, Jesse had been good to Asher. He'd always looked out for him as a friend, not just a security guard, and having Jesse back felt like a little piece of his old life was still there. A sense of normalcy.

Asher stopped pacing. "Happy?" he asked with a smirk.

Jesse laughed. "Quite."

Asher smiled. He didn't like how the events of tonight had unfolded, but he knew the outcome had been achieved and everyone was coming home safe.

Jesse said "Copy," and Asher realized he had an earpiece in.

"Do you wear them all the time now?" Asher asked when it appeared the conversation was over.

"Earpieces? Yes. It's the best way to communicate throughout the palace. We'd trialed them before, but we'd always had tech issues. But these earpieces are good," Jesse said, then quickly added, "Except in tunnels, evidently."

"Evidently," Asher said, his anger still lingering, and Jesse didn't miss it.

"I get why you feel the way you do, Ash," Jesse said. "But they achieved something I don't think our team would've ever been able to do. This is why they have the reputation they do—they achieve things no one else can. Recently, they took down an organized crime unit that multiple agencies around the world had been trying to destroy for years. People are still talking about it. They say James Thomas can do the impossible, and that's why I suggested bringing him in."

Jesse sighed. "I know I've been under investigation, Ash. And likely still am—even being here tonight might've been a test. And as hard as that's been, given how long I'd worked for your father and how long I've been your bodyguard, I understand it. If they didn't investigate me, I'd honestly be concerned. I haven't liked being kept in the dark, but it's not about liking what they do. It's about getting results, and I couldn't have gotten you the results they did tonight. So when he comes in here, go easy on him. Especially when you see Abi," he said with a slight grimace.

Asher frowned. "What's that supposed to mean?" he asked quickly.

Jesse sighed. "She's covered in Lamberi's blood, and James is concerned you're going to lose it when you see her. She's not hurt, and the last thing she needs after tonight's ordeal is for you to be arguing with him. So, when she comes in, take her to the living suites and let her clean up. James needs to debrief with his team and Samuel and then we're going to meet up in the morning."

"Okay," Asher said heavily. He'd dealt with enough tonight, and in all honesty all he wanted was time with Abi.

"Good," Jesse said, sounding pleased with himself. Asher wondered if he'd been expecting a fight.

Asher heard the garage door open and Jesse reached for the door handle.

"Copy," Jesse said. "Wait inside," he told Asher, as if Asher had a choice—Jesse was standing in his way.

The door eventually opened and James walked in first. Even Asher had to admit he looked like hell. He had a cut on his jaw, multiple scrapes on his arms and one arm was covered in blood. Asher didn't know if it was his or someone else's.

Rachel followed, and then Abi—on crutches again.

Asher's stomach churned when he saw her, but he remembered Jesse's words. He forced himself to stay calm.

She looked up, smiling when she saw him.

He tried his best to return her smile, but he couldn't draw his gaze away from her neck and chest. There was even blood splattered over her face.

He took her hand, drawing her in. "You're going to give me a heart attack one day," he whispered in her ear.

She gave a small smile. "Don't worry, I have no desire to go on any more adventures with James Thomas."

Asher smiled fully now, kissing the crown of her head.

"Come with me," Asher said, needing to wash that blood off her.

Asher released her, only so she could move.

He saw James talking quietly to Jesse, who was nodding in return. Asher liked that they were communicating.

James looked over to him, as if sensing he was being watched.

"Thank you," Asher said.

"You're welcome," James responded with a nod.

Asher turned back to Abi. Lamberi was dead, and now she would be able to sleep at night without fearing him in her dreams.

"Let's get you cleaned up," Asher said.

Security followed them to their living quarters and scoped the suite before they were allowed in. Security stayed outside the door.

Asher led her into the bathroom. Once again Abi was injured and back from hell, but this time it felt different. This time it felt like a new beginning.

He closed the door behind them and locked it. Her back was still healing and he didn't want the hot water to sting her wounds, so he wet a small towel with warm water.

"Come here," he whispered, his voice gruff.

She stopped in front of him and he wiped the towel over her neck.

He brought his lips to hers and drew her in. She melted in his arms and her tongue swept over his. He closed his eyes, savoring every moment.

Asher cupped her ass, drawing her in, pressing their bodies flush.

She kissed him faster, hungrier, and he gave her everything back.

"I was so scared of losing you," he whispered, pulling back to kiss her neck. He wanted to kiss everywhere Lamberi had touched her.

"And I was so scared Lamberi would punish you for my escape," Abi said, meeting his eyes.

"I would've paid the price, Abi. I would've paid it a million times over," he said.

Her eyes glistened. "I know, but I didn't want that for you. Besides, I couldn't live the rest of my life looking over my shoulder, worried when he would come for me."

Her eyes dropped down to her bloody T-shirt. Asher lifted it and pulled it over her head, throwing it on the bathroom floor. She stood tall, not embarrassed, and he loved that. He removed her bra, grabbed a clean towel and wiped away the final remnants of Lamberi's blood. Then he threw the towel on the floor beside her stained T-shirt.

His lips ran over her collarbone and she tilted her head back, opening her neck to him.

Asher groaned as her chest rose and his lips trailed between her breasts. His thumb brushed over her breast and her nipple hardened beneath it.

Her breath grew heavy and Asher's body ached in response.

She looked up at him with wanton eyes. "Make me forget about Lamberi—about killing him and about being held captive. I want to forget it all."

Asher's hands ran through her hair and his mouth crashed down on hers. "I'll make you forget everything but me," he promised, his voice low and thick.

A moan fell from his lips and his cock hardened.

His hands went to her hips but he took his time. He kissed her until he was breathless, and then he kissed her until she was panting.

His fingers trailed the soft skin of her waist, stopping on the top button of her jeans. He paused, looking into her eyes.

She nodded and he fought to keep control.

"Not here," he said, lifting her into his arms. He carried her into the bedroom, grateful security were still outside the living quarters, and sat her on the edge of the bed.

She lay back but Asher didn't miss the slight wince.

"I'm fine," Abi said quickly.

"You're not fine," Asher said, taking her arm, pulling her up.

But she shook her head stubbornly.

"Don't," she said gently. "I'm fine. I really am."

Asher didn't have it in him to resist. "You have no idea how much I want you," he told her, his voice husky.

He lay over her, holding his weight on his elbows. She grabbed his hips, pulling him closer. Her sweet lips brushed over his and any lingering concerns for her back left him. He needed this—they needed this.

He was hard and aching for her. Throbbing.

She lifted her hips, grinding into him, knocking the breath from his lungs.

A guttural groan fell from his lips and he could barely think straight. His mouth consumed her, kissing her like he'd never kissed before. Heat spread through his body, and he felt alive.

"I need you," she whispered, but she had no idea just how much he needed her.

"I'll take care of you," he whispered, a promise. He'd take care of her in the bedroom, and out of the bedroom. Any way she needed. Forever.

He placed kisses from her neck to her shoulder and between her breasts. She arched her back and he swore under his breath.

Her hard nipples were visible through her lace bra and his mouth went to one, flicking it gently with his tongue and then sucking it harder. Abi moaned in response and he pulled the lace down, taking her nipple in his mouth. She sucked in a sharp breath and lifted her hips—a silent beg for more.

His hand ran over her tight stomach and down to her jeans. He undid them and kneeled, sliding them off. He took a moment to take her in.

Her white lingerie and her willing eyes made her look angelic. Some might argue Abi was far from angelic, but to him she was. She was pure and good and he wanted every inch of her.

She followed his gaze as it swept over her body. Her hair was sprawled over the bedding, messy yet beautiful.

She raised an eyebrow and her lips parted. Asher swore under his breath then lowered to his knees. He spread her legs wide, opening her to him. He kissed the sensitive skin of her inner thighs, teasing her. She shuddered and Asher smiled as his lips continued to please her.

He ran a finger between her wet folds, his cock thick and hard, begging to enter. He forced himself to go slow, to give her everything she needed, to make her forget the past few weeks and focus only on him.

He ran his tongue over her clit and she bucked against him. Her hands threaded through his hair, tugging it, setting the pace. He licked and sucked her as she rocked against his face. Her voice was hoarse and the sweet pant from her lips drove him wild. She shuddered, and he knew she was close.

He sucked harder as he pushed two fingers deep inside her. She was so wet and hot he couldn't think straight, and he could barely remember what he was supposed to do.

Abi screamed his name and he licked her softly as she came around his fingers, clenching them tight.

When she settled, he stood, stripping his clothes at a speed he was sure he'd never done before. Her eyes heated, and the corners of her lips turned up.

He hovered over her and she parted her lips. He thrust his tongue in, giving her a taste of her own sweetness. "Abi," he moaned as he lifted her. He lay down, propped up by pillows and she climbed onto him, straddling his lap. Their eyes locked as she lowered onto him. Asher sucked in a breath and his eyes rolled back, closing.

He groaned, deep and guttural, biting his lip as she rode him.

His fingers dug into her hips, slowing her down, because if she continued at that pace Asher didn't think he'd last a minute.

She leaned forward, her breasts brushing against his naked chest, her lips finding his. She sucked his earlobe and whispered in his ear. Asher wasn't even sure what she was saying, but he liked it anyway. Everything about her felt good.

He rocked against her, pushing in deeper, needing to feel all of her.

She was his, and only his. No one was taking her from him.

Never again.

He grabbed one breast, guiding her nipple into his mouth. It was full and swollen and heavy and he closed his eyes, relishing in the moment before moving to the other one.

"You're so wet," Asher groaned, slapping her ass as she rocked against him.

"Whose fault is that?" she asked, panting in his ear.

"Come here," he said, cupping her cheek and guiding his mouth to hers. He kissed her hungrily as he rocked harder, slamming his throbbing cock into her hot pussy. She tightened around him and he almost came.

He swore again and she kissed him harder.

Their bodies were slick with sweat and their breaths frantic and panting.

She was blowing his mind and he gave in, releasing all control.

She responded, grinding harder and faster, her clit rubbing against his pelvic bone.

She was so hot and tight and he still couldn't get enough of her.

"Baby," he whispered as he cupped her ass, pushing deeper. He felt his orgasm building and her hot kisses on his neck were driving him wild.

"I'm going to come," she moaned, almost a whimper.

"Come on me," he commanded. He was right on the edge, right there with her.

He felt the moment she released, clenching around him so tightly his body exploded, every nerve alive and firing.

He held her tight, grinding against her until they both settled. Once they were still, he didn't let her move.

"Stay here for a moment," he whispered, and she laid her head on the pillow beside him, kissing his neck.

He closed his eyes as he held her, basking in the warmth of his orgasm.

He wanted this forever.

He wanted her forever.

He wanted her to be his queen.

ABI

*H*is ragged breathing settled and his hands caressed her skin, leaving a hot trail in their wake. She lazily pressed her lips to the soft skin of his neck. Her body felt light and heavy at the same time, and her head was spinning, but she'd never felt happier.

He gave a sated groan as he closed his eyes.

She took a moment to watch Asher without him realizing. He looked peaceful and content. His jaw was soft and relaxed and the steady rhythm of his heart told her he'd needed this as much as she had.

He'd told her he'd make her forget, and that he'd take care of her, and he'd done exactly that.

"What?" he asked with a hint of a smile that told her he knew she was watching him.

"Nothing," she said. Her voice seemed to have that post-sex glow that people said came after. Abi was sure they'd meant post-sex skin glow, but her voice seemed to have absorbed that.

"Nothing?" he asked, raising an eyebrow.

She chuckled. "That was everything I'd ever hoped for. If I'd known you were going to be that good in bed I'd have ripped your clothes off the second I met you."

Asher's chest rumbled as he laughed. "What am I going to do with you?" he mused.

"I have a few good ideas," Abi said coquettishly, wiggling her eyebrows as she propped herself up on her elbows.

Asher tilted her chin to his, brushing his soft lips over hers. His lips were surprisingly soft and tantalizing.

Asher's eyes widened suddenly. "I didn't even think to ask you. I just assumed you're on birth control."

"Relax," Abi said, "I am. I think the last thing you need right now is a baby to complicate things."

He seemed thoughtful. "Not right this second," he said, searching her eyes. "But someday. Santina needs an heir," he said, and then his expression turned thoughtful. "Well, the heir could become one of my cousin's children. But I'd like it if it was my own."

She smiled. "I want children, Asher."

His hands went to her hips and his thumbs spread over her stomach. Abi didn't even know if he realized he was doing it. "One day," he whispered, his eyes locked on hers.

It was two words, but in that moment she knew they meant more than that. It was his commitment, his promise of their future. And despite her concerns of whether she was right for him, she wanted him. She wanted to walk beside him every day. She wanted to be there for him if everything seemed insurmountable. She wanted to be his queen, and to serve Santina.

The silence between them became electrified, and she lowered her mouth to his.

He kissed her again, but this time it was different. It was a promise.

"I will take care of you, Abi," he said.

She'd never thought of herself as someone who needed taking care of—she'd always been the one to take care of others—but there was something about Asher's promise that made her heart warm.

"And I'll take care of you," she said, looking deep into his eyes.

He seemed to stop breathing for a moment. "Forever," he whispered, his throat thick.

"Forever," she said, placing a lingering kiss on his forehead.

Forever.

Their moment only lasted a second before a knock on the door interrupted them. By the sound of the fist banging, it wasn't good news.

Asher swore under his breath as Abi climbed off, tucking herself under the sheets. Asher strode to the bathroom, grabbing a robe before opening the door. James stood with his fist up, ready to smash down the door.

"What?" Asher asked, his tone sharp—likely sharper than he'd intended.

However, James didn't seem to care one bit.

"You need to look at something," he said.

Asher was silent a moment. "Give me a minute," he finally said, resigned.

Asher closed the door and returned to the bed. He leaned over, cupping her cheeks. "Stay here and get some rest. I'll be back as soon as I can."

"Okay," she said. "Wake me up if you need anything."

His lips lingered on hers and with a heavy sigh he pushed off the bed, dressed and left.

The suite was quiet and Abi didn't hear any arguing voices outside the door. She didn't know if that was a good thing or not.

She pulled the blanket up to her chin and exhaled a soft sigh. Asher had given her the release she'd been craving and, as she closed her eyes, she felt the pull of sleep take her.

ABI OPENED HER EYES, rubbing them. The bed beside her was empty.

She put a hand on the crumpled, cold sheets.

Had Asher come to bed at all last night?

Abi sighed, desperately needing a shower. She found a fresh towel in the bathroom and a stack of clean clothes that someone—perhaps her mom—must've picked up from her apartment. But first she remembered the little white pill in her jeans. She grabbed it, relieved when she found it still tucked in the pocket. She flushed it down the toilet, not wanting anyone to accidentally ingest it thinking it was something else.

Then she turned on the shower and stepped in, letting the hot water run over the front of her body. She kept her back dry and protected. It wasn't the best shower of her life, but regardless it felt so good.

She turned on the television as she dressed. She rummaged through her makeup bag until she found a bottle of foundation.

And then it fell from her hands, shattering on the bathroom floor as her head snapped to the television.

The death toll continues to rise after last night's terrorist attacks.

Abi couldn't breathe as she watched the blackened and destroyed city hall filled with frantic first responders helping out the injured.

370 are dead, and hundreds more are unaccounted for.

She stepped over the shattered bottle and ran. Security was alert as she rushed out of the living quarters.

"Where is he?" she asked.

"Asher is in his office," one of them responded, but she was already running in that direction.

James was standing outside, talking on his cell phone when Abi arrived. He opened the door and her heart sank into the pit of her stomach when she saw Asher hunched over his desk, his face buried in his hands.

"I'll keep you informed," someone said over the telephone.

"Thank you," Asher responded, ending the call as he looked up at Abi.

She fought to keep her face impassive but his bloodshot eyes and drained face made her heart stop.

"Maybe Santina will fall after all," he said, hanging his head in his hands. The despondency in his voice was heartbreaking.

She rushed to him.

"No," she said, taking his hands, forcing him to look at her. "You don't believe that and neither do I. Santina will not fall, not on your watch."

"It wasn't enough," he said through gritted teeth. "They're attacking anyway. Thomas Security stopped a few of them, but they couldn't stop all of them."

Abi touched his jaw, guiding his face back to hers. "Now we fight back," she said, locking her eyes on his.

This time he didn't look away. This time she saw fire in his eyes, and that was a hell of a lot better than defeat.

"James!" Asher called, suddenly.

James entered as if he'd been approaching before Asher had called him in.

Abi noted the white envelope in his hands. He'd been holding it outside, looking at it while he'd been on the telephone, but she hadn't had time to think it through.

"What's that?" Asher asked.

"A letter from Colonel Stevens," James responded.

ASHER

"From the colonel?" Asher asked, his eyebrows weaving together.

James nodded. "Sit down," he said before giving Asher the envelope.

Asher hadn't realized he'd stood, but admittedly his mind was a mess. He didn't like being told to sit down, either—nothing good ever followed that command.

James hesitated and then passed him the envelope.

Asher unfolded it, noting it was a handwritten letter. "Have you verified this?" he asked, not wanting to read it until it had been.

James nodded. "Yes. It arrived at the palace about an hour ago, and Samuel verified it a few minutes ago. It must've been written shortly before his death. We're still trying to work out why there was a delay in it being delivered through the post."

Asher's hands trembled slightly. Abi stood beside him with her hand on his shoulder.

Asher drew a deep breath and prepared himself for what he knew was going to be more devastating news.

Dear King Asher,

I write this letter with great regret—regret that I did not send this letter to your father. I have asked myself time and time again if I could've prevented his death had I passed on what I have seen and heard.

These accusations are unfounded, but I know I have wasted too much time already and perhaps you are the only one who can verify them.

Santina is bleeding from the artery.

I have seen things—small clues—that caused me to watch some members of our military more closely. I fear this has garnered me too much attention, but that is a price I am willing to pay. Your father loved Santina, as do I.

Six months ago, I was in the wrong place at the wrong time. I saw something I was never meant to see, and something I spent months wishing I hadn't seen.

I saw Henry Walter in Santina, and he was not alone—Alistair was with him.

I do not know what was spoken about at the meeting, but it did not look like a friendly discussion. This was the first sign that something was perhaps wrong, but I could not be sure. Henry Walter has a unique role to play in this world; he is often called in to clean up "messes" that governments can't be seen dealing with. I wanted to give Alistair the benefit of the doubt, but now I fear that was a fatal decision.

There is one military unit you need to watch carefully— 104Raiders. They disappear at times and talk in hushed whispers. These things alone are not for grave concern, but they speak of a man I do not know, and cannot find.

Martin Snider.

I have heard whispers about him, but I cannot find out who he is. He is Santinian, of that I am sure. I think the name is an alias, that he is someone who does not want to be known. All the same, his name raises the hairs on the back of my neck.

A few nights ago, I received a telephone conversation from Martin Snider. His voice sounded familiar, but I couldn't place it. He asked me for one thing: allegiance to the Santina Revolt.

I do not know specifically what this Santina Revolt is, and the questions I have asked have not been well received, but this is something you should know about, and you should use whatever means necessary to destroy it.

Find Martin Snider, and you will find the root of this revolt.

If something were to happen to me before you read this, please know that I gave my life willingly to protect our beloved Santina.

Yours faithfully,
Colonel Stevens

Asher stared at the letter. While it mostly confirmed what they already knew, it gave him one important truth: Alistair was still lying.

Asher looked to James. "Bring Alistair to me."

James left without a word.

Asher stood, moving toward the large windows that looked out onto the garden.

We fight back.

Abi's words repeated in his mind—that letter couldn't have come at a better time. A few minutes ago he'd been overwhelmed and didn't want the responsibility of his title.

But it was *his* title, and no one could do this but him.

The colonel had given his life for Santina, and Asher would do the same if he had to. But for now, all he had to do was fight.

Jesse had round one with Alistair, and Asher would have round two, because Asher knew all the buttons to push with his brother.

"I'll come back," Abi said.

Asher shook his head. "Stay," he said, knowing her presence would only help to unravel Alistair. When Alistair had brought up Asher's involvement in IFRT, there had been something in his eyes—hatred, perhaps—and Asher didn't think it was all aimed at IFRT. He couldn't imagine what Abi would've done to him, but maybe it was what she hadn't done. Asher thought that Alistair hated the fact that Asher had been able to date Abigail Bennett, and then convince their father to support the relationship. Abi should've been off limits to both brothers.

Abi stood behind his desk, watching him carefully.

He walked over, cupped her cheeks, and then kissed her forehead. His lips lingered, never ready to let her go.

Asher heard a knock on the door before it swung open and Alistair, disheveled and dirty, was led in by James. His hands were cuffed and by the marks around his ankles, Asher knew his legs had been bound too.

He stared at Alistair, but no guilt came to the surface of his mind. Alistair had dug his own grave and as far as Asher was concerned, he had Noah's and their father's blood on his hands.

Alistair threw a foul look Asher's way, but it took him a second to realize Abi was there. When he did, his eyes flared, confirming everything that Asher suspected. To her credit, Abi didn't flinch but she did look uncomfortable.

"Brother," Alistair said, his voice laced with contempt.

"Sit down," Asher said.

"A couch. What a privilege," Alistair said with a crooked smile.

"I instructed security to give you the same treatment Abi was given. I'm assuming you don't like it," Asher said calmly.

If looks could kill, Alistair would've pierced his soul with the look in his eyes, and it took Asher aback for a moment.

"What happened to you?" Asher asked.

Alistair scoffed. "Don't play innocent, Asher."

"Innocent? I'm not *playing* anything, Alistair," Asher said, his voice cutting. "I'm giving you one final chance to tell me what you've been doing. If you don't, I'm going to have you executed on charges of treason. You have five minutes to convince me otherwise," Asher said, his heart breaking as he said the words. He truly understood how his father had felt convicting his own brother of fraud. He'd imprisoned him for life, though, rather than executing him, but Asher didn't have a choice. Anyone involved in the murder of King Martin had to face execution.

"Why is she here?" he said, not looking at Abi.

"Because she will be queen, and palace business is now her business," Asher said.

"You will never be queen," he said, looking straight at Abi.

"That is Asher's decision, not yours," Abi said.

Anger flashed in Alistair's eyes, and he returned his attention to Asher. "If you knew the truth about her, you would never make her queen."

Asher fought to remain impassive. "What truth?" he asked calmly.

Alistair stared at Asher, and finally said, "Perhaps it's best for you to find out on your own." He shrugged.

Asher refused to let Alistair get under his skin. If Abi wasn't who he knew she was, Thomas Security would've told him otherwise. This had to be another play by Alistair, because Abi was just another target to him.

"You're not here to talk about Abi. You're here to tell me about your meeting with Henry Walter, and your relationship with Martin Snider," Asher said. "Give me something to work with, Alistair. Don't force my hand."

Asher dragged a chair over to the couch and sat so that he was at eye level with Alistair. He positioned the chair back far enough that Alistair couldn't lunge at him, even though James was sitting beside him, poised like he was ready for an attack.

"Contrary to what you think, I went to the meeting with Henry Walter with good intentions. He's a disease, and I thought nothing good could come from his presence in Santina," Alistair said, sounding like himself for the first time since he'd been dragged in.

"What was discussed at this meeting?" Asher asked.

Alistair chuckled scornfully. "I went on the pretense of finding a new dealer," he said. "I was playing dumb, just trying to break the ice and get him to think I was an ignorant, drug-addicted prince. I mean, that wasn't much of a stretch, was it, Asher? You thought the same."

Asher raised an eyebrow. "Actually, no I didn't. Everyone thought you had the potential, but had made a run of bad decisions. You brought that upon yourself, so don't be a martyr."

"Don't be a martyr," he repeated with a strained laugh. "Life is so easy for you, isn't it? Everything has been handed to you."

"*Handed* to me?" Asher asked, his voice raising. "Would you stop thinking of yourself for a minute? Look at my fucking life! I lost my brother—my best friend—and my father in a matter of weeks. I'm being attacked and undermined from every angle, including by my own family, and my patience is running out. You have three minutes to start talking, Alistair, or I swear to God this will be the last conversation we ever have!"

Asher was shaking, but he kept his hands in his lap to hide it. His anger, and the emotions he'd been suppressing all night, were bubbling to the surface and a small part of him was scared he'd kill Alistair himself.

"Fuck you, Asher!" Alistair spat, his eyes wide with rage. "You think I'm the bad guy? You think I killed our father? If you knew me at all, you would know I'd never do that."

"You sold holy land, forged our father's signature, and you were the only person who knew when they were leaving on the morning they were killed. What am I supposed to think?" Asher asked through gritted teeth.

"I didn't know," Alistair said. "I didn't know what was going to happen!" His gaze returned to Abi. "Get her the fuck out of here."

Asher lost control, and he grabbed Alistair's shirt. "If you ever speak to her like that again—"

James stepped in, putting a hand on Asher's chest. "Talk, Alistair. My patience is wearing thin, and I'm not as nice as Jesse. I'll shred you into pieces if that's what it takes to get the truth."

Alistair shrank back at the menacing tone of James's voice. Asher did the same, even though it wasn't directed at him. Asher wondered in that moment what James was capable of, and then decided he didn't want to know.

"I didn't have a choice," Alistair said, his expression suddenly breaking down. "Martin Snider has my child, and he's going to kill him if he finds out that I even told you that," Alistair said hoarsely. "For once I was trying to do something good, something unselfish . . ." He looked down and shook his head. Asher had never seen him appear so broken. "And I still managed to fuck it up."

"You have a child?" Asher asked, his voice a whisper.

"DNA results came back positive," he mumbled, still not looking up. "I knocked up someone on a wild night out. She kept the baby, of course—she thought she was going to raise the future heir of Santina. But after the succession changed, and she realized this kid was never going to be king, she lost interest in him. She's a fucking junkie, worse than I am. Martin Snider stepped in, paid her money, and she gave him up. Now he has him, and I'm at his mercy. You can think what you want of me . . . but everything I've done has been to protect him."

"You should've come to me," Asher said, his words pained. "I would've helped you." His mind reeled—he knew now why the little boy in the photographs on Noah's computer looked familiar: because he looked like Alistair, and Noah had known.

"I went to Father," Alistair said bitterly. "He told me I made the mess and I needed to sort it out on my own."

"I don't believe that," Asher said. He couldn't believe that his father would neglect to help his own grandson. "What exactly did he say?"

"Who?" Alistair asked like he had no idea what they were talking about.

"Father! What did he say about your child?" Asher asked. It was then that he noticed the beads of sweat across Alistair's forehead. "Jesse told me you were clean. But look at you—you're still in withdrawal."

Asher looked to James, but he didn't look surprised by this revelation. His expression didn't change at all.

Asher's mind was spinning and the conversation was going in circles. He would get the name of the boy's mother and let James deal with that problem. Right now, he needed answers.

"How did Martin Snider help you negotiate the deal for the ruins if you'd never met him?" Asher asked.

"He called my cell phone, and sent me the paperwork in an envelope addressed to the palace. He told me to get it velvet stamped and it was a done deal," Alistair said simply.

Asher paused, the blood in his vein froze over like he'd been thrown into the Antarctic. "What did you say?"

"What?" Alistair said.

"You said velvet stamped," Asher said slowly.

Alistair's eyebrows threaded together. "So?"

"Are you sure?" Asher asked.

Alistair seemed thoughtful for a moment. "Yes. What's strange about that?"

Asher suddenly knew who Martin Snider was, and he felt sick to his core.

"The official term is chopped and stamped. I've only ever heard someone say velvet stamped, because it was a joke—a reference to our father and his love of velvet."

Alistair frowned, indicating he'd had no idea.

Asher looked to James.

"Find my cousin Troy. Bring him to me," Asher said.

James's black eyes darkened and he left without another word.

"What does Troy . . ." Alistair's voice trailed off. When he looked to Asher, his teeth ground together. "No," he whispered.

Asher stared out the window to the palace gardens beyond—a place his father had spent hours walking, clearing his mind.

"What are you going to do?" Alistair asked.

"I'm going to execute him," Asher said, turning to stare his brother in the eye. "And then I'm going to destroy Adani. The world is going to see who they really are. I'm going to take everything from them, just like they tried to do to me.

"I'm going to destroy them all," Asher said as a fierce determination rose in his chest. "Adani will fall—and I'm going to take it."

THE STORY CONTINUES...

The third, and final, book of The Royals will be released in April 2020.

* * *

In the meantime, click here to download a FREE copy of *ESCANTA*, Book One of the James Thomas Series.

ALSO BY BROOKE SIVENDRA

THE JAMES THOMAS SERIES
    Escanta
    Saratani
    Sarquis
    Lucian
    Sorin
    The Favour

THE DEACON THOMAS DUET
    The Ranger
    The Redemption

THE THOMAS SECURITY SERIES
    The Vault
    The Traitor
    The Conspirator

THE SOUL SERIES
    The Secrets of Their Souls
    The Ghosts of Their Pasts
    The Blood of Their Sins

DID YOU ENJOY THIS BOOK? YOU CAN MAKE A BIG DIFFERENCE

Reviews are the most powerful tools in my arsenal when it comes to getting attention for my books. As much as I'd like to, I don't have the financial support of a New York publisher. I can't take out full page ads in the newspaper or put posters on the subway (not yet, anyway).

But I do have something much more powerful and effective than that, and it's something those publishers would kill to get their hands on.

A committed and loyal group of readers.

Honest reviews of my books help bring them to the attention of other readers.

If you've enjoyed this book I would be so grateful if you could spent just a few minutes leaving a review (it can be as short as you like) wherever you bought the book.

Thank you so much.

ABOUT THE AUTHOR

Brooke Sivendra lives in Adelaide, Australia with her husband and two furry children. She has a degree in Nuclear Medicine and worked in the field of medical research before writing her first novel.

You can connect with Brooke at any of the channels listed below and she personally responds to every comment and email.
www.brookesivendra.com
brooke@brookesivendra.com
Facebook: www.facebook.com/bsivendra
Twitter: www.twitter.com/brookesivendra
Instagram: www.instagram.com/brookesivendra
Pinterest: www.pinterest.com/brookesivendra

Lightning Source UK Ltd.
Milton Keynes UK
UKHW011833181221
395882UK00001B/248